THE MAN FROM CHEYENNE WELLS

When 60,000 dollars are taken from the bank at Cheyenne Wells, two of the raiders are killed, and the third, Vance Brady, serves a prison sentence. However, the money was never recovered. On release from jail, Brady decides to go straight and to help the widows of the two dead men by sharing the money from Cheyenne Wells. During his search for the two women he finds a place to settle down but soon runs foul of a bounty hunter and men with designs on the money. Can Brady overcome his difficulties in going straight?

THE MAN FROM
CHEYENNE WELLS

The Man From Cheyenne Wells

by

Floyd Rogers

Dales Large Print Books
Long Preston, North Yorkshire,
BD23 4ND, England.

British Library Cataloguing in Publication Data.

Rogers, Floyd
  The man from Cheyenne Wells.

  A catalogue record of this book is
  available from the British Library

  ISBN   978-1-84262-698-6 pbk

First published in Great Britain in 1964 by Robert Hale Ltd.

Copyright © 1964 Floyd Rogers

Cover illustration © Gordon Crabb

The moral right of the author has been asserted

Published in Large Print 2010 by arrangement with
Mr W. D. Spence

Dales Large Print is an imprint of Library Magna Books Ltd.

Printed and bound in Great Britain by
T.J. (International) Ltd., Cornwall, PL28 8RW

Chapter One

Vance Brady stirred the embers of the fire and pulled his short woollen jacket tighter around him. The light was fading from the sky and already the chill of night was in the air in the high country to the west of Cheyenne Wells. The flames flickered revealing a weather-beaten, rugged but handsome face and deep blue eyes which stared thoughtfully at the fire. He sat for a few moments then pushed himself to his feet, turned up the collar of his jacket and stood listening as if wanting to hear the sound of an expected visitor.

No sound broke the silence of the Colorado country. He stamped his feet trying to drive some warmth into them, then kicked a log on to the fire sending a shower of sparks into the air. He strode up and down, his hands deep in the pockets of his fawn trousers which were tucked into the top of worn, but obviously comfortable, calf-length boots.

There was still a faint light in the western

sky when the quiet clop of horses' hoofs caused Vance Brady to freeze in his step. He listened for a moment then swiftly and silently, almost snake-like, he moved away from the light of the fire to the side of a huge boulder. He drew his Colt from its worn holster and the weapon seemed to become part of him. He crouched, balanced perfectly on his feet ready for instant action.

The horses drew nearer and two figures emerged from the darkness carefully picking their way amongst the boulders and rocks into the hollow.

'He's already here,' said one of the riders. 'That's his horse.'

Recognising the voice Vance relaxed, pushed his Colt back into its leather, drew himself to his full height of six feet and stepped from the shadows.

'Howdy, Ace,' he called.

'Hi, Vance,' greeted Ace enthusiastically as he swung from the saddle and slapped Vance on the shoulder with his left hand whilst his right grasped Vance's in the firm grip of long standing friendship. 'It's mighty good to see you.'

It was three months since the two men had met and now at this pre-arranged meeting they were glad to see each other again.

'See you still got the same outfit,' laughed Vance, stepping back and looking Ace up and down.

'Sure,' grinned Ace, 'it suits me.'

He was dressed completely in black; a black shirt, covered by a black vest, was tucked in the top of black levis now dusty with travel. His black curly hair with long side-winders showed thickly from beneath a black, shallow-crowned, wide-brimmed sombrero. His features were smooth, his face long and thin but his eyes sparkled as if he enjoyed life.

'You always did believe in being conspicuous,' said Vance.

'Why not, we never found it made any difference,' replied Ace, 'besides it's something like a trade-mark with me.' He noticed Vance looking past him at the young cowboy who still sat on his horse. 'I'm sorry, Vance,' he went on heartily, 'I should hev introduced you before but seeing you again, well–' He left the sentence unfinished, and half-turned. 'Climb down, Tom,' he called, 'an' come an' meet the great Vance Brady, slickest drawer of a gun I've ever seen, the man with the coolest brain in the West and the greatest bank-robber of them all!'

'Cut it out,' muttered Vance as the cowboy stepped from the saddle and walked forward with his hand outstretched. Vance took the hand firmly and recognised in the return grip a little nervousness. 'Don't take any notice of him, Tom,' he added.

'Mighty glad to know you,' replied Tom. 'Surname's Corby.'

Vance watched him carefully, seeing a young man whom he estimated was barely twenty. He had a round, boyish face, browned by the sun and the wind. His clothes betrayed him as being a cattle drover and he carried himself as if trying to pass off an experience greater than his years, as if trying to impress the man with the reputation. Vance knew he lacked experience for the job he had in mind and he wondered why Ace had picked him up.

'Pleased to meet you, Tom,' said Vance. 'No need to tell me you're from Texas, your voice gives you away.'

Tom grinned. 'I've heard a lot about you although you never worked down there.'

'Don't believe all you've heard about me,' advised Vance. 'Git some coffee an' we'll rustle up a meal.'

'Good idea,' agreed Ace. 'We sure could do with something to warm us up.' He took the coffee pot from the fire and poured some into two mugs. He passed one to Tom who took it gratefully.

Vance started to prepare a meal and, after they had finished their coffee, Ace and Tom unsaddled their horses and laid out their bed-rolls for the night. By the time they had finished Vance had bacon and beans almost ready.

Tom came close to the fire and, when he squatted on his haunches, Vance handed him a fork.

'Keep your eye on thet,' he said. 'I want to have a look at my horse.'

Tom nodded and Vance pushed himself to his feet. As he walked towards his horse he looked at Ace who was walking towards the fire. Vance signalled with an inclination of his head and Ace followed him. When they reached the horse Vance turned to Ace.

'What's the idea of bringing him along,' he asked, keeping his voice low. 'I guess he's never pulled a job before; all he knows is cattle.'

'Liked the look of the boy, an' he's in trouble,' replied Ace.

'What sort of trouble?' queried Vance.

'Not with the law,' answered Ace.

'Thought not,' said Vance. 'I don't want to lead anyone on to the wrong path. I'll talk to him.'

He started to turn away but Ace arrested him by grasping his arm.

'Hold on, Vance,' he said, 'he's in worse trouble than the law – wife trouble!'

'Wife trouble?' Vance was astonished. 'He's too young.'

'No he's not,' replied Ace.

'Then why does wife trouble make him want to turn bank robber?' asked Vance.

'I picked him up in Nebraska, in Ogallala,' Ace explained. 'He'd helped push a herd up from Texas; he'd got separated from his outfit after they had been paid; got into a card game an' lost all his money; things got a bit rough but I managed to pull him out all in one piece.'

'But we can't be takin' on any drover thet loses his pay,' said Vance.

'Let me finish,' said Ace. 'Jest before he came north he got married, his pay was goin' to help them set up a home; I expect he thought he could increase it at the card tables, wal – the professionals took him fer a ride. I took pity on him; thought you wouldn't mind splitting three ways especially when it was goin' to make two people happy at the start of their married life.'

'You always had a sentimental streak,' grinned Vance.

'Come an' git it!' Tom yelled.

'All right, be there in a minute,' shouted back Ace. He turned back to Vance. 'Give him a break.'

Vance looked thoughtful. 'He's a raw kid fer this job.'

'With us two around he'll be all right,' said Ace. 'If we leave him here I can't see him accepting charity when we git back.'

'Guess he'd be too proud for thet,' agreed Vance. 'All right, he comes along. We'll brief him after we've eaten.'

The two men strolled back to the fire where Tom had everything ready. They enjoyed the meal and after it was over Vance looked at Tom across the fire.

'You sure you want to go through with this, Tom?' he asked.

'Certain,' answered Tom. 'I need the cash but apart from thet I'll be able to tell my children that I once worked with the great Vance Brady.'

'Look, Tom,' said Vance seriously, 'there is nothing big in workin' with me, I'm on the wrong side of the law an' if we pull this job you will be if you're caught – wal–'

Tom laughed. 'We won't be caught. Vance Brady's never caught. No lawman has ever had his hands on you, but I guess with a price on your head in three states there are some thet sure would like to.'

'All right,' said Vance, 'now listen carefully to what we tell you, do as we say an' everything will be all right.' He glanced at Ace and nodded.

Ace grinned back then looked at Tom. 'Although Vance is the fastest gunman in the West he's never drawn his gun in anger on a lawman. Oh, you'll find eighteen notches on his gun but not one wore a star, an' every one was in self-defence. That way he's only wanted for robbery an' those wanted posters declare thet Vance Brady is wanted alive.'

'Remember thet carefully, Tom,' said Vance. 'We don't shoot to rob, we try and pull these robberies without a shot but if we have to shoot we only do so to scare or give us a chance to git away.'

Tom nodded. 'I'll remember,' he said.

'Where is it to be?' asked Ace.

'Cheyenne Wells,' replied Vance. 'Nice and handy to here, lucky we picked this meetin' place when we parted three months ago.'

'Thet's the way we work,' explained Ace turning to Tom. 'After a raid we part for three months, this foxes any posses an' we hope thet there might be a job to pull near our pre-arranged meeting place.'

'I've been around here for four days,' explained Vance, 'an' I've got wind thet the bank in Cheyenne Wells will be holdin' a large deposit tomorrow.' He glanced at Tom. 'When we split after this raid you hit the trail fer Texas an' thet pretty wife of yours as fast as you can an' fergit thet you ever rode with Vance Brady.'

Vance went on to outline his plans for his raid on the bank in Cheyenne Wells.

The following day the three men were up early, and after breakfast they broke camp, saddled their horses and were soon riding at a steady pace towards Cheyenne Wells.

It was late morning when they rode into the small Colorado town. The sun shone brilliantly from a cloudless sky and it was so hot that there were only a few people in the dusty main street. The three men rode slowly as if this was just an ordinary visit to town. They pulled up outside the salon, tied their horses to the rail, strolled casually inside, and crossed to the long mahogany counter where Vance called for three beers. They lounged against the bar enjoying the cool drink. Vance glanced around the room and saw that there was only a handful of cowboys at the tables. When they had finished their beer they strolled outside and leaned on the rail, surveying the street. The sheriff's office was in the next block and just beyond that stood the bank.

Vance glanced at Tom Corby and noticed that he was eyeing the proximity of the two buildings with some misgiving.

'Don't worry about thet, Tom,' whispered Vance. 'You know the plan; keep to it and everything will be all right. No matter what happens stick to us and don't panic.'

Tom nodded and licked his lips nervously. He wished he felt as calm as his two companions appeared to be. He stepped to his horse and untied a cloth bag from the saddle.

'It's almost noon,' said Vance as he pushed himself from the rail. 'Let's go.' He turned along the sidewalk in the direction of the bank.

The three men walked casually along the sidewalk, and on reaching the bank they walked straight inside without looking round. Tom stopped beside the door whilst Ace accompanied Vance to the counter.

A clerk looked up as they approached. 'Good-day, gentlemen,' he said brightly. 'You are just in time; we were about to close for lunch. What can I do for you?'

In one movement both Vance and Ace

drew their Colts swiftly from their holsters and the clerk's eyes widened with surprise and fright when he saw himself staring into the cold muzzles of the guns.

'You can open the safe,' said Vance calmly as Ace moved swiftly round the counter and menaced the manager and second clerk with his gun.

The manager hesitated but when he felt the hard steel pressed into his ribs he backed to the safe. He fumbled for his keys and Ace waited impatiently whilst he unlocked the safe. As the door swung open Ace brought the barrel of his Colt sharply down on the back of the manager's head. The official fell to the ground without a moan.

'Right,' called Vance and, as prearranged, Tom hurried to the safe and quickly emptied its paper contents into the bag. At the same time Ace dealt with the two clerks, leaving them unconscious on the floor.

'All ready?' asked Brady.

The two men nodded and Tom handed the bag to Vance.

When they reached the door Ace stepped outside and when he did not reappear Vance and Tom knew that the street was clear. Tom strolled out to join Ace, and Vance, after removing the key from the inside of the door, walked outside, closed the door and locked it. Pocketing the key he joined Ace and Tom.

'Wal, if anyone comes to the bank now and finds it locked they won't suspect anythin'; it's after closing time,' he said. 'We'll hev a good start before anythin' is discovered.'

They set off casually along the sidewalk towards their horses tied outside the saloon. Vance glanced at Corby. He saw the boy was nervous and his eyes were darting everywhere.

'Keep calm, Tom,' whispered Vance. 'Be natural.'

At that moment a man stepped out of the sheriff's office. He paused, looked along the street, then started in their direction.

'Sheriff!' There was a frightened note in Tom's voice as the word hissed from his lips.

'Steady, Tom,' said Vance.

Ace moved forward in front of Vance to allow the sheriff to pass. The lawman was naturally curious about any stranger in town and, as he approached the three men, he took a good look at them.

Noticing the way the sheriff was eyeing them Tom panicked.

'He's on to us,' he gasped, terror seizing him.

His hand flashed to his gun and jerked his Colt from its holster. The sheriff was taken by surprise by the action of the men in front of him but always alert he was not slow to react to Corby's movement. As Tom's gun came up the sheriff's Colt was already breaking leather.

Vance had noticed Tom's action and, reacting quickly, he swung his bag knocking Tom's arm upwards as he pressed the trigger. The shot, which shattered the stillness of Cheyenne Wells, whined harmlessly upwards. The action jerked the bag open and some of the paper money flew on to the sidewalk.

The sheriff, with his gun already out, sized up the situation in a split second. He squeezed the trigger and lead crashed into Corby's chest sending him spinning backwards against the wall. Everything had happened so quickly that Ace never really knew what was happening and as soon as his first shot was fired the sheriff swung the gun on the man in black and squeezed the trigger again. Ace halted in his step as if he had hit a wall; his hands clutched at his stomach and he pitched forward on to the boards.

Vance was galvanised into action at the sheriff's first shot. He leaped past Ace but was too late to save him. He was on top of the lawman before he could bring his gun to bear on Vance who swung his fist hard and true to the sheriff's jaw. The lawman staggered backwards against the rail, lost his balance and fell into the roadway unconscious. Brady raced for his horse and by the time he reached it people were already running from the saloon. He was in the saddle in a flash and as he turned the animal he glanced back at his two companions but he realised they were beyond his help. He stabbed his horse with his heels and the animal bound forward and broke into an earth-pounding gallop along the main street. He gained a few precious yards before anyone realised what was happening with a result that their firing was ineffective.

The sheriff was struggling to get up when two men ran up and helped him to his feet. He shook his head trying to clear it, then staggered to a nearby water-trough, bent over and plunged his head into the water. The coolness helped to clear his head and as he straightened up he started yelling orders.

Two men ran to the bank whilst the rest raced to their horses and in a matter of a few minutes a posse, with the sheriff at its head, was thundering out of Cheyenne Wells in pursuit of Vance Brady.

Chapter Two

Vance Brady flattened himself along his horse's back and called to the animal for greater effort. He glanced anxiously over his shoulder as he tore along the west road away from Cheyenne Wells. There was no sign of pursuit but he knew it would be only a matter of a few minutes before a posse was on his trail. The dust billowing from the flashing hoofs would give his position away and he realised his only chance would be to out-ride the posse to the hills where he hoped to be able to give them the slip. A second glance behind him told him he had not much of a lead for the tell-tale cloud of dust indicated a group of horsemen leaving the town at a fast gallop.

After ten minutes' hard riding Vance saw that the distance between himself and his pursuers was no greater. He knew if he reached the hills the sheriff would stick grimly to his task of trailing and hunting him down, therefore he reckoned that he would have to court capture to outwit the posse and make his escape. The rugged country and darkness would then be his allies.

Earth flew as the horse stretched itself along the trail which cut across the grassland rising gradually to the hill country. Estimating the distance ahead carefully, he eased his pace, encouraging the posse into an eager, blind pursuit. When he reached the hills Vance kept to the main trail which twisted and turned through the rougher countryside.

After rounding two sharp bends Vance suddenly hauled his mount to a sliding halt. He turned the animal and put it at a narrow cutting in the hillside. The ground sloped steeply but the powerful horse took it in its stride and Vance pulled to a halt behind a group of boulders. He slid from the saddle quickly and held his horse steady, soothing it with softly spoken words. He was not a moment too soon; the posse, urged on by the fact that they were closing the gap, thundered past, missing the tell-tale marks of Vance's halt.

As soon as they were out of sight Vance was back in the saddle sending his horse down to the trail. He knew he had not much time; it would not be long before the sheriff realised that their quarry was no longer ahead of them. He turned his horse back along the trail in the opposite direction to the posse and kept the animal at a fast pace for two miles before turning into the hills in a southerly direction. He held his horse to a steadier speed as he worked his way across the country from valley to valley and across rolling expanses of hills. He cast many an anxious glance behind him but saw no sign of pursuit and as darkness began to envelope the countryside he felt reasonably safe.

When Sheriff Matt Owen saw the bank robber's pace slacken an urge of triumph went through him. They would soon make a capture and the money would be back at the bank before nightfall. Eagerly anticipating success he urged his horse faster and the animal stretched itself along the dusty trail with the rest of the posse pounding close behind. They had gained a few yards by the time they reached the hills and the sheriff realised that the man ahead might give them the slip unless the gap was closed rapidly. Once again his horse answered his call for a greater effort and he was somewhat relieved when they were able for the most part to keep the man in sight.

It was only when the trail twisted sharply for a considerable distance that they lost sight of their quarry but the sheriff reckoned that at the pace they were maintaining there would be little chance for the thief to slip off the trail. So intent was he on closing the gap that he pounded round the bends without thought for signs on the ground.

Two miles further on the trail straightened and when the posse galloped into this section they realised the bank robber was no longer ahead. The sheriff slowed his horse and when he pulled to a halt the other men milled around him.

'Given us the slip,' he yelled. 'We'll hev to work our way back an' try to pick up his trail.'

The men spread out and gradually worked their way back the way they had come. It was only after some difficulty that the posse picked up Brady's trail. They could follow it only slowly and darkness was closing round the hill country when they lost the trail again. The sheriff called a halt.

'I reckon it's no use trying any longer tonight,' he said, disappointment in his voice. 'We've been moving so slowly that he'll be miles away. We'll git back to town an' I'll circulate his description through the State.'

Somewhat dejectedly the sheriff led his posse back to Cheyenne Wells.

It was a sad and lonely man that made camp that night deep in the hills to the south west of Cheyenne Wells. If only he had stuck to his first impressions; it had been against his better judgment that he had agreed with Ace to let Tom Corby in on the raid and now both of them were dead. He felt that somehow or other he must make up for what had happened and, as he sat sipping his coffee and staring into the fire, an idea came to him. In the stillness of the Colorado night sleep did not come early to Vance Brady as he turned over the idea in his mind.

He was awake early the following morning and, as he prepared breakfast, he reassessed the plan he had made during the night. Satisfied with what he had in mind he broke camp and headed southwards. He realised that by now his description would be circulating through the State and the authorities in Cheyenne Wells would have received word that this description fitted the wanted Vance Brady. He would have to be extra cautious and, thinking that the sheriff from Cheyenne Wells may have picked up his trail in daylight, he kept doubling back on his tracks until he was satisfied that no one could follow.

It was early evening when he came in sight of the small town of Lamar and, realising he dare not enter the town in daylight, he waited in the hills to the north west until darkness covered the Colorado countryside.

He entered Lamar at a walking pace and made his way through the side streets until he was at the back of a large house which stood a little apart from its neighbours. Vance tied his horse to a rail and stepping over the low white fence hurried towards the house. He flattened himself against the wall and paused to make sure that no one was about. Satisfied that all was quiet he edged his way along the wall towards the window from which a light was shining. Brady paused against the window then inched forward until he was able to peer through a chink in the curtains.

A man of about fifty-five, smartly dressed in a fawn frockcoat and matching trousers, was sitting in an easy chair smoking a cigar and reading a paper. As far as Vance could see there was no one else in the room. He circled the building and seeing no more light in the house reckoned the man was alone. Vance stepped on to the veranda and rapped sharply on the front door. A few moments later the door was opened by the man whom Vance had seen through the window. He held an oil lamp and as the light fell on Brady his eyes widened with surprise. The man opened his mouth to speak but before he could do so Vance pushed his way past him into the hall.

'What on earth are you doing here?' asked the man angrily, shutting the door quickly.

Vance smiled. 'Take it easy, Mister Griffith,' he said quietly. 'Are you on your own?' The man nodded. 'Anyone likely to call?'

'Shouldn't think so,' replied Griffith.

'Then I think we'd better hev a chat,' said Vance.

Without a word Griffith led the way into the room where he checked the curtains. It was only when he was satisfied that he turned back to Brady who was warming himself in front of the fire.

'What do you want?' he snapped. 'Don't you realise there's a price on your head in this State after what happened in Cheyenne Wells yesterday?'

'I thought there might be,' smiled Vance.

'I expected you'd be over the border by now,' went on Griffith, pacing the floor nervously. 'If anyone saw you come in here I'd be finished.'

'Calm down,' soothed Brady. 'No one saw

me arrive, I made sure of that.'

'Well, state your business and get out of here quick,' snapped Griffith irritably.

'Jest some more cash to put to my account,' explained Vance.

'I can't handle that money!' Griffith faced Vance angrily. 'When we made our arrangement I thought it was understood that you wouldn't operate in Colorado.'

'I think you're mistaken, Mister Griffith,' said Vance. 'I agreed not to raid your bank if you held an account for me. I said it was unlikely that I would work in Colorado but the bank at Cheyenne Wells was holding a special shipment and it was too good to miss.'

'But ... but ... I daren't touch that money,' spluttered the bank manager.

'You will,' said Vance and he opened the bag he was holding. He put his hand inside and threw some bundles of dollar bills on to the table. 'Check it,' he ordered.

Griffith stared wide-eyed at the money, then glanced round sharply as if he feared that someone was watching them. He rushed up to the table, scooped up the bundles, and hurried to a safe in one corner of the room. As he put the money into the safe he counted the bundles and slammed the door shut as quickly as he could.

'Ten thousand dollars!' said Griffith nervously.

'Good,' said Vance. He looked hard at the bank manager. 'See it gets into the correct account,' he said meaningly. 'Vance Webb, remember?'

Griffith nodded. 'Now get out of here,' he said, 'and be careful you are not seen. Another thing, Brady, can't we close this account soon?'

Vance grinned. 'Does it embarrass you?' he asked. 'Don't worry, with what I hev in mind I might close it sooner than you think.'

'Good, good,' said the bank manager as he started to hustle Vance to the door. 'Now, please go.'

Vance stepped into the hall and crossed to the front door. He was about to open it when Griffith jumped forward in front of him.

'Don't be a fool,' snapped the bank manager. 'Let me have a look, there may be someone about.'

Vance laughed and stood to one side. Griffith opened the door slightly and peeped outside. Satisfied there was no one in the immediate vicinity he stepped on to the veranda, and a moment later signalled to Vance.

Brady hurried out of the door and with a chuckle bade the bank manager farewell before walking briskly round the house to his horse.

As he rode away he smiled to himself at the thought of a bank manager nervously mopping his brow and pouring himself a large glass of whisky to try to ease his nervous encounter with a bank robber. Brady headed westwards at a brisk pace and with the moon shining from a clear sky the trail to La Junta was easy to follow.

It was half-past ten when he reached the town which he circled to reach a long, low house. He pulled to a halt in a small group of trees a short distance from the dwelling, slipped from the saddle and secured his horse to one of the trees. He saw that lights were burning in three rooms and through one of the windows, across which the curtains had not been drawn, he could make out several people.

Vance cursed softly. Establishing contact with the bank manager of La Junta was not going to be as easy as his previous visit, but he could not afford to wait; he wanted to keep moving and get out of the State as soon as possible. He took the bag of money from the saddle and hurried stealthily towards the back of the house. A light shone from the kitchen window and creeping forward Vance saw a Chinese cook preparing a meal. He moved to the back door and, after pausing long enough to pull his neckerchief over the bottom half of his face, stepped inside, drawing his Colt as he did so.

Although the cook opened his mouth to shout the sudden appearance of a masked man shocked him so much that no sound came out. Vance was beside him in a flash.

'No sound, and you'll not get hurt,' he hissed, pressing his Colt hard into the man's ribs. The man was shaking with fright and all he could do was nod. 'Is there a party on?' asked Vance. The cook nodded again. 'Go and tell Mister Logan thet there is something you want to see him about in the kitchen.' The man nodded once more and turned to go but Vance stopped him. 'Don't say anything about me to anyone or I'll blow your head off.' The Chinaman shrank backwards terrorised as Vance shoved the muzzle of the Colt into his face.

He hurried away and a few moments later Vance heard him returning with the bank manager who was protesting loudly at being taken away from his guests. When Logan entered the kitchen he stopped in his tracks staring wide-eyed at the masked man menacing him with a gun.

'What's this?' he gasped. 'Who are you? What do you want?'

'Get rid of him,' snapped Vance indicating the cook.

The bank manager knew from the tone of voice that it was no use meddling with this man. He nodded to the cook.

'Go and see if the table is set for the meal,' he ordered.

The cook moved towards the door but Vance stopped him. He stepped forward menacing the Chinaman with his Colt.

'Don't try to give the alarm,' he hissed, making his voice sound threatening, 'or else I kill both you and Mister Logan.'

'I won't, I won't,' replied the frightened cook and shot through the doorway.

Vance started to chuckle, pulled his neckerchief from his face and slid his Colt into its leather.

'You!' gasped Logan. 'What's the idea breaking in here like this?'

'I saw that you had guests and I figured you wouldn't want me coming to the front door,' replied Vance.

'Certainly not,' spluttered the bank manager. 'What a night to come,' he nodded in despair. 'I've got the judge in there, if he should...'

'He won't,' interrupted Vance. 'My business is short and sweet.' He opened his bag and extracted some bundles of money. He counted as he dropped them in front of Logan who stared in amazement. 'Ten thousand,' said Brady. 'See that they go into my account, wal, Vance Webb's account to you.'

'But I can't handle that,' protested Logan, 'if it's from Cheyenne Wells.'

'It is,' said Vance, 'and you'll handle it when you remember our little agreement.' He turned towards the back door, paused and picked up a chicken from the table. 'I'm sure you and your friends won't mind if I enjoy this under the stars.' He stopped outside then turned. 'I'm sure you'll see that your cook mentions nothing of my visit.'

Vance shut the door and quickly made his way to his horse, leaving the bank manager's brain in a turmoil as he stared at the ten thousand dollars lying on his kitchen table.

Brady had planned to make his call on the bank manager of Rocky Ford fifteen miles to the west the same night, but he was feeling tired after a long day in the saddle and he was also tempted by the chicken which he had acquired. He made camp beside a stream five miles north of La Junta and, after an enjoyable meal, he rolled himself in his blanket, keeping his Colt and the money close beside him.

The next morning he headed across country to Rocky Ford, timing his arrival for nine o'clock when he knew the bank would be opening. He did not want to wait until darkness and reckoned that with some care his presence in Rocky Ford would go unnoticed. He turned up the collar of his jacket and pulled his sombrero down over his forehead, hiding his face as much as possible. He rode steadily so as not to attract attention and once he reached the bank he was out of the saddle and into the bank quickly. The clerks were busy preparing for the day's work. Without hesitation Vance crossed to the door marked 'Manager', tapped sharply, and stepped swiftly into the room.

'Good heavens!' gasped the bank manager, almost falling off the chair with surprise. 'You've a nerve walking into here in broad daylight after what happened at Cheyenne Wells.'

'That's why I'm here,' said Vance. 'I won't mince words, there's ten thousand dollars;

put it into Vance Webb's account.' Brady threw the bundle of bills on to the desk.

The bank manager stared at them for a moment then quickly swept them into a drawer when there was a tap on the door. He looked up at Vance, alarm showed in his eyes.

'Anyone see you come in?' There was a frightened note in his whisper.

'Your clerks,' replied Vance, 'but I don't suppose they saw my face.'

'Keep your back to the door,' instructed the bank manager. 'Come in,' he shouted in answer to a second knock.

A clerk opened the door and stepped into the office but hesitated when he saw there was someone with the manager.

'I'm sorry,' he apologised. 'I didn't know there was someone with you, sir.'

'That's all right,' answered the bank manager trying to sound natural, 'but come back in five minutes, Mister Webb is about to leave.'

The clerk backed out of the office and as soon as the door closed the bank manager jumped to his feet facing Brady with some annoyance on his face.

'Get out of here quick. I'd be ruined if this was found out.'

'May be you won't hev my account fer long,' replied Brady.

'Settle thet later,' answered the manager. 'Just go, now, you're too hot to be around here.' Vance turned to the door. 'No, not that way,' called the bank official irritably, 'use my private door.' He showed Vance to a door which led on to a side street.

Brady hurried round the corner to his horse, swung into the saddle and, deeming it better to leave Rocky Ford unnoticed, turned up the side street and made his way towards the edge of town. He was relaxing in the saddle, pleased that he had almost gained the outskirts when a man walked round the corner. Vance gasped when he saw the tin star pinned to the brown shirt.

The sheriff was equally surprised when he saw a man fitting the description which he had received yesterday. His hand was moving towards his gun when Vance kicked his horse forward and the sheriff had to leap to one side to avoid the flashing hoofs. Brady turned the corner and was protected from any gun shots by the buildings. He guided his horse skillfully, tore on to the edge of Main Street and thrust the horse into an earth-pounding gallop away from Rocky Ford.

The sheriff scrambled to his feet and raced after Brady. When he reached the main street he fired after the horseman but he was out of effective range and the lawman used the shots as a means of attracting his deputy. When he saw him run from the office the sheriff yelled to him to bring the horses. The deputy unfastened the reins, swung quickly into the saddle and brought the two horses racing towards his superior. The animals had not stopped before the sheriff grabbed the reins and leaped into the saddle as he sent his horse forward.

'Vance Brady!' yelled the sheriff.

The lawmen urged their animals faster as they pounded out of Rocky Ford on the trail of the bank-robber whose horse was sending a cloud of dust billowing behind it giving away its position.

As the earth flashed beneath the flying hoofs Brady looked behind him. He saw two horsemen heading out of town in fast pursuit and he called on his horse for greater effort. When he glanced behind him again a few minutes later he saw that he had not widened the gap between himself and his pursuers and he knew he was going to have a hard ride if he was going to shake off these two determined lawmen. He swung gradually towards the foothills of the towering Sangre de Cristo Mountains hoping that in the rougher country he would be able to lose his pursuers and cross Raton Pass into New Mexico.

The pace was fast but as the countryside rose steadily towards the distant mountains the going became harder and the speed slackened. Vance crossed from one ridge to the other, moved up one valley, down another, flanked one hill, avoided another but even though he used every trick he knew he could not shake off the Sheriff of Rocky Ford and his deputy. He began to realise that the riding of the past two days, coupled with the rough terrain and the heat, were taking their toll on his horse. Gradually the lawmen were closing the gap!

Brady turned to rougher country, climbed steep slopes, pressing his horse hard and with every step drew nearer to Raton Pass. He was ever looking for an opening which would enable him to outwit the men on his trail but he could find none. He knew if he turned to fight he could easily have the drop on them but he realised that once he did this and turned his gun on lawmen he would be doomed for the gallows.

In the early afternoon he climbed to a ridge on the other side of which he saw a large shallow valley. Close to his right a little below the ridge there was a great upheaval of boulders and beyond them in the hillside the entrance to a cave. He glanced behind him and saw the lawmen were starting up the slope. His horse was about spent and he knew he would never outrun his pursuers across the long valley. He pushed his horse forward below the skyline and turned towards the cave. When he reached the entrance he glanced back anxiously but the sheriff and his deputy had not appeared. He must be rid of the thirty thousand dollars which he still held and away from the cave before they realised he had been there. He slipped from the saddle quickly and close to the cave's entrance found a recess in the rock face. He pushed the bag containing the money as far back as it would go then hurried back to his horse, climbed wearily into the saddle and sent the tired animal down the slope, heading along the valley.

He knew that once he topped the steep slope at the far end there were two more rough ridges to cross to reach Raton Pass, but he figured he would never make it; the lawmen were already pushing their horses down the slope and the gap had closed considerably. Suddenly, as if sealing his fate, his horse faltered, the pace slackened and then the animal limped to a walking pace. Vance knew the horse had gone lame. He pulled to a halt, slid from the saddle, patted the horse's neck, and got down on one knee to examine the injured leg.

Vance straightened slowly to face the lawmen who were heading rapidly towards him. He raised his arms and a few moments later was relieved of his Colt and was a captive of the law for the first time.

Chapter Three

'Brady, you have been with us nearly five years; in that time you have been a model prisoner, with the result that I have obtained the permit for your release tomorrow – six months' remission for good conduct.'

The grey-haired governor of the state penitentiary looked up at the prisoner standing between two guards on the opposite side of the large oak desk. He saw a man who had changed little in the five years he had spent in prison. The governor, used to reading men, had realised that, when the twenty-three-year-old bank-robber had been brought before him to start his first prison sentence, he had a man who was determined not to let prison life get on top of him. Now at twenty-eight Vance Brady looked little older than that first day.

A gleam of pleasure showed in Brady's eyes at the news. His thoughts raced, to be outside these walls, to breathe the free air, to ride far and wide, to see the rolling grasslands and high mountains, to feel the wind and the rain; the things he had dreamed about over the past years were to become a reality! Vance had done some deep thinking whilst in prison; he realised how much he had missed these simple things and he was determined not to lose them again.

'You are a man with intelligence above the usual run of prisoners, and I believe because of this you outwitted the law for so long and had the sense to see that to shoot it out with lawmen would only lead to the gallows and that that was why you saved the life of the Sheriff of Cheyenne Wells.' The governor paused momentarily, stared at his hands thoughtfully, then looked Brady straight in the eye. 'Therefore, I am going to offer you some advice and I hope you have sense enough to take it. Don't go back to the life you have known; there is so much that is worthwhile; return that money and start afresh.'

'I appreciate your advice, sir.' Brady spoke softly. 'I have already made up my mind to go straight but I cannot return the money. I doubt whether I will be able to lay my hands on it again.'

He paused, and seeing the governor was about to speak he added hastily, 'Don't ask me what I intend to do with it if I get it but there are certain things I must take care of.'

The governor looked hard at Brady. He knew better than to press the matter.

'Well, I'm glad to know you mean to go straight,' he said, shrugging his shoulders, 'but let me add a word of warning. You realise that it is generally known that the money was never recovered and if my guess is correct there'll be more than one person on the look-out for you, hoping to get their hands on a fortune. Also, there is still a price on your head in three states, so watch out for bounty hunters.' The governor rose slowly from his chair and extended his hand. 'Good luck, Brady, I shan't see you in the morning but the only things you had when captured, your clothes, gun and horse, will be ready for you.'

Vance took the governor's hand in a firm grip. 'Thank you, sir,' he said.

The two guards escorted the prisoner from the governor's office to the cell block where Brady spent his last night in prison making plans for the future.

The following morning he was given his clothes and when he was ready he was taken from the cells to his horse. He smoothed the horse's neck gently and spoke as if the intervening four and a half years had never happened.

The guard handed him his gun belt and as Vance took it he looked at it thoughtfully. There were no bullets in the belt and he knew without checking that there would be none in the gun. He fastened the belt slowly round his waist, and checked the hang of the gun before tying the leather thong round his thigh to hold the holster firm. Vance straightened and flexed his fingers two or three times. Suddenly he crouched, perfectly balanced on his feet. His right hand flashed downwards and in one swift movement, almost too fast for the eye to see, the Colt appeared in his hand. The guards gasped in amazement at the speed of the draw. Vance Brady had lost none of his old swiftness with a gun.

He slipped the Colt back into the holster, unfastened the thong, unbuckled the belt and without a word to anyone stuffed it into his saddle-bag.

Vance led his horse from the stable to the prison gate where the guard swung it open and wished him luck as he passed through to the outside world. The door clanged behind him and he paused for a few moments enjoying his new-found freedom. He swung into the saddle and sent the horse forward at a steady trot, getting pleasure from the movement of the powerful animal beneath him.

Brady rode steadily throughout the morning until he reached the outskirts of the small town of Boulder. He pulled to a halt outside an old shack, slipped from the saddle, but received no answer to his knock on the door. He turned back to his horse and rode slowly down the short, dusty main street until he reached the saloon. After hitching his horse to the rail he swung through the squeaking batwings and it was no surprise when he saw the man he wanted standing at one end of the bar with a glass of beer in front of him.

Vance strolled slowly towards him studying him carefully. Charlie Murphy had not altered a great deal, maybe there were a few more lines around his eyes but they were still sharp and clear. His creased, weather-beaten face was partially covered by a thick grey beard and drooping moustache. His clothes were worn and dusty and Vance guessed that he still had not struck it rich, in the mountains beyond Boulder.

Brady stopped beside the old man. 'Howdy, Charlie,' he said with a smile.

Charlie, who was staring at his beer, glanced up and his vacant look was suddenly split by a grin of surprised recognition.

'Vance Brady! Why, you old son-of-a-gun,' he cried. He gripped Vance's hand and slapped his shoulder in friendly greeting. 'When did they let you out?' he asked.

'Just today,' replied Vance. 'I've come straight here.'

'Wal, you're a sight fer sore eyes,' said Charlie. 'Sorry that last trip of yours went wrong,' he added seriously. 'But they don't seem to hev done you much harm in the pen.'

'I was determined they wouldn't,' answered Vance who then called for two beers.

'I was sorry about Ace,' said Charlie. 'I couldn't figure how you got jumped thet day.'

Vance looked thoughtful, a far-away look

came into his eyes. 'Poor Ace,' he muttered, 'it was all because he did someone a good turn an' persuaded me to help.' Brady paused, then turned suddenly and looked at Charlie. 'I'll tell you about it some day but I'd rather not talk about it now. I came because I need your help, Charlie.'

'Sure,' replied the old man. 'Anythin' I can do… You've always been good to me an' I never fergit it.' Suddenly he caught sight of Brady's waist. His eyes widened with surprise. 'No gun?' he gasped.

Vance smiled. 'No,' he replied. 'I'm goin' straight; I'm not losing my freedom again. I reckoned I'd be better without a gun but I realise I was wrong; I'm goin' to need it very soon even if I don't press the trigger in anger. I can see a little job comin' up but after thet off comes the gun-belt.' He laughed when he saw the puzzled expression on Charlie's face and went on to explain. 'Two hombres hev been tailin' me ever since I left the prison. Only the law knew about my release so I figure they are a couple of agents hopin' I'll lead them to the Cheyenne Wells money. Wal, I figure I'll hev to get them off my back so I might hev to do a little shootin' to scare them.'

'Where do I come in?' asked Charlie.

'I need some cash,' answered Vance. 'I'll need some ammunition, also I'd like to fix myself up with a few things as I reckon I'll be doin' a lot of long hard ridin' seein' I'm goin' to head for Texas.'

'Texas!' Charlie was surprised. 'But you...'

Vance grinned. 'Don't try to talk me out of it,' he said. 'I've something to attend to down there. Now what about some cash, can you manage it?'

'Sure,' said Charlie. 'I'm always takin' a little yellow dust out of the mountains; never hit a bonanza but jest enough to keep me goin'.' He pulled a wallet from his pocket and passed fifty dollars to Vance. 'Thet do you?'

'More than enough,' replied Brady. 'Thanks a lot, but it's only a loan.'

'Fergit it,' said Charlie. 'Anythin' else I can do?'

'Maybe,' said Vance. 'Did you see Ace between our last two raids?'

'Yes,' replied the old man. 'Spent a week here.'

'Do you know anythin' about his family?' asked Vance. 'We worked a lot together but we never asked about each other's past; we figured it better to take each other as we were an', as you know, it helped form a great

47

partnership. Now I wish I knew something about his family.'

Charlie stroked his beard. 'Then you didn't know that six weeks before the raid on Cheyenne Wells Ace got married in Denver?'

'What!' Vance gasped with surprise. 'He never told me, but then we had little time together before Cheyenne Wells an' maybe he figured if he'd said anything I wouldn't hev operated with two married men.' Vance's lips tightened in annoyance and despair. 'Why didn't he tell me? I'd hev called it off and he'd hev still been alive.'

'I saw him the day before he set out for Cheyenne Wells,' said Charlie. 'He said he didn't want to let you down an' thought he would tell you after the job.'

Vance said nothing for a few moments and there was sadness in his eyes as he thought of Ace's loyalty.

'Do you know where his wife is?' asked Vance.

''Fraid not,' answered Charlie. 'They were married in Denver but I believe she came from Greely.'

'Know her name?' queried Vance.

'Della,' said Charlie, 'but thet's all I know.'

'Thanks,' said Vance. 'At least I've got

48

somethin' to work on.' He called for two more beers and whilst they were enjoying them two men with the dust of the trail upon them entered the saloon.

Charlie eyed them shrewdly. 'I think your friends hev joined us,' he whispered.

Vance, who had his back to the batwings, heard the men walking towards the bar and when they reached the counter he glanced casually in their direction.

'Sure hev,' he muttered.

'Can smell their type a mile off,' snorted Charlie.

'They look thirsty, but I don't think I'll give them time to hev a beer,' grinned Vance. 'Come on, Charlie, I've some things to get an' I'm ready for a meal.'

He pushed himself from the bar and together with Charlie left the saloon. They strolled down the sidewalk and as they turned into the store saw the two men come out of the saloon and lean on the rail. Vance ordered several necessary items for his travel and said he would collect them after he had eaten. The two men were still outside the saloon when he and Charlie crossed the street to the café. After the meal Vance collected his gun-belt from his saddle-bag, an action which was not lost upon the two agents, and returned to the store. When he reappeared on Main Street with his goods, his gun-belt, fully equipped with ammunition, was strapped around his waist. After loading his horse he bade goodbye to his old friend, climbed into the saddle, and as he headed out of Boulder he observed his followers step down from the sidewalk and mount their horses.

With these two men following him, Vance thought it wisest to head in the opposite direction to Greely so that his intention of visiting that place would not be known. He kept to a steady pace, moving in a south-westerly direction looking for a suitable place at which to deal with his pursuers. About eight miles from Boulder the trail took him over the spur of the hill, then dropped through a narrow cutting between two high shelves of rock. Once in the cutting Vance urged his horse forward quickly and when he reached the other end where the trail dropped gradually into a wide valley he turned his horse off the trail, slipped from the saddle and moved back quickly to the end of the cutting. He drew his Colt from its holster and tensed himself in readiness for the appearance of the two men.

He had not long to wait before the clop of

hoofs on the hard ground announced their approach. They came out of the cutting cautiously and Vance, hiding behind some rocks, waited until they were clear of any cover. He was about to move when the two men pulled to a halt.

'He's not in sight,' said one, glancing round.

'He must be around here somewhere,' said the second.

They swung slowly from their horses, secured them and, looking round, cautiously moved away from the animals. Immediately they were free from cover Vance stepped into the open, covering them with his Colt.

'Hold it!' he snapped. Taken by surprise the two men froze in their tracks. 'Unbuckle your belts,' ordered Vance. 'Easy like, an' keep your hands clear of those guns.' Seeing it was useless to argue with the cold steel pointing in their direction they did as they were told. The gun-belts clattered on the hard ground. 'Kick them over here,' rapped Vance.

The men shoved the belts towards Brady who stepped forward and kicked them further out of reach. He studied the men thoughtfully for a moment.

'You,' he said, indicating the taller of the

two agents, 'lie face downwards with your hands behind your back.' Reluctantly the man did as he was told and when he was prostrate on the ground Vance turned to the other man. 'Get your lariat,' he snapped. The man shuffled to his horse and when he came back with the rope Brady told him to tie his companion's hands. 'Then pull his feet up behind him towards his hands and tie all four together,' he went on.

When the task was done Vance ordered the free man to lie down and he tied him up in a similar manner. Satisfied with the security of the ropes Brady straightened and looked down at the two men.

'Wal, I guess you'll be able to get together, somehow, work on each other's ropes an' eventually get free, but it will take you some time back to back an' by thet time I'll be far away,' Brady grinned.

He hurried to his horse, removed his gun-belt and, after putting it in the saddle-bag, rode quickly away in the same direction as he had been travelling. Once out of sight he began to swing in a wide circle until he was heading towards Greely.

It was early evening when he rode into the town and pulled up outside the hotel. He slipped from the saddle and entered the three-storey wooden building. The lobby was spacious with a bow-shaped reception desk behind which a clerk was sorting some papers. Three people were sitting in one corner and a group consisting of a man, two ladies and a young woman of about twenty-three were standing near the desk.

'I'd like a room for the night,' said Brady when the clerk looked up.

'Certainly, sir,' he replied. 'Room twelve, just sign the register, please.'

Vance picked up the pen and wrote his name in the book whilst the clerk took the necessary key from the board.

'I wonder if you can tell me if there is a Della Jenkins living in Greely?' asked Vance as he took the key from the clerk.

The man pursed his lip thoughtfully. 'Can't say that I know of anyone of that name,' he replied. 'Sheriff might be able to help you.'

Vance smiled, muttered his thanks, and walked to the door unaware that the young lady standing with her mother and father and aunty had been startled by his question.

She glanced sharply at her parents and was somewhat relieved that they had been too deep in conversation to hear the query. She studied Vance closely as he crossed the lobby and returned a few moments later with his belongings.

As Brady hurried up the stairs the clerk glanced at the name in the register. His eyes widened with surprise when he read the words. 'Vance Brady!' he gasped to himself. 'Maybe I'd better warn the sheriff.' He started to move from behind the desk but another customer detained him and Vance had reappeared before the clerk was free.

'Which direction for the livery stable?' asked Vance.

'Hundred yards to the left, Mister Brady,' spluttered the clerk, a look of bewildered fright in his eyes.

Vance grinned. 'I see you know me,' he said, 'but there's nothing to worry about, I'm goin' straight now.'

The clerk seemed to visibly relax as a wave of relief spread over him. 'Well, I'll try and make one or two enquiries about the lady you want, Mister Brady,' he said going out of his way to sound obliging.

'Thanks,' said Vance and hurried out of the hotel.

The young lady had been startled to learn that the man enquiring about Della Jenkins was Vance Brady, the notorious bank robber, and was so preoccupied with her thoughts that her father spoke to her twice before she realised it.

'Come along,' he said. 'Stop your day-dreaming, Fay, we're going home. I've left a message for your uncle to follow.'

Once outside the hotel she stopped.

'Daddy,' she called. 'You go along, I want to see Tom. I'll get him to walk me home in a few minutes.'

'Very well,' said her father and hurried after his wife and sister-in-law.

Fay turned across the street as if making for the sheriff's office to see Tom Heston, but then turned back to the hotel where she waited impatiently in the lobby.

When Vance re-entered the hotel a short while later Fay jumped from her chair and hurried to meet him.

'Mister Brady,' she said as she confronted him. 'I would like a word with you, Fay Carlyle's my name.'

Vance was taken aback at this approach by a young lady in a town where as far as he knew only the clerk knew his name. He looked curiously at Fay.

'Certainly, miss,' he replied, removing his sombrero, 'Shall we sit down?'

The girl smiled and led the way to two chairs in a corner.

'How did you know who I was?' asked Vance as they sat down.

'I'm afraid I overheard you and the clerk talking,' she replied. 'I know it was wrong of me to listen but I heard you question him and my curiosity was aroused.'

'My question...?' Vance started, then suddenly realised to what she was referring. 'You know Della Jenkins?' he asked eagerly.

The girl nodded and looked anxiously round the lobby as if afraid of something.

'Is anything the matter?' asked Vance.

'Well, I'm supposed to be seeing Tom Heston, the deputy sheriff,' explained Fay. 'That's the excuse I made to my father to come back to see you. If he knew I was here talking about Della Jenkins there would be trouble.'

'Trouble?' said Vance mystified. 'I think you'd better tell me the story from the beginning.'

'Della was my best friend,' said Fay. 'When she was eighteen she married Ace Jenkins against the wishes of her family. She was gloriously happy but for some reason her parents did not take to Ace. It was only after the raid on the bank at Cheyenne Wells that she knew he was a bank robber; he'd told her he was going on a cattle deal. Her parents would not take her back, they were rather narrow and strict and Della wandered away from Greely.'

'Do you know where she is?' asked Vance.

'Three years ago I had a letter from her; she was in Wagon Mound in New Mexico. I gathered from her letter that she had been having a hard time, but she told me nothing of what she was doing. My father supported Della's parents and forbade me to have anything to do with her. I wrote to her and explained the situation. She has appreciated and respected my awkward position and I have not heard from her again.' She paused, sadness in her eyes. 'I've longed to have news of her and often wished I could help her but...' She left the sentence unfinished but Vance knew the difficulties she would have encountered. 'Why do you want to see her?' she asked.

'I did not know of Ace's marriage until this morning,' explained Vance. 'If I had known before Cheyenne Wells I would have insisted on Ace stepping down. I felt I must try and find his wife and help her if I could.'

Fay rose from her chair. 'I must go, Mister Brady, I have told you all I know,' she said, 'but if ever you find Della, please give her my love and tell her there is never a day goes

by but that I think of her and our friendship.'

'I certainly will, miss,' replied Vance. 'And
thank you for your help. May I escort you
home?'

'Thank you,' said Fay, 'but I'd better call
on Tom.'

As Vance watched her leave the hotel he
wondered if he would find Della Jenkins the
same girl as Fay remembered.

Chapter Four

Vance Brady left Greely the following morning and throughout the succeeding days
moved steadily southwards avoiding all
human contact. He remembered the governor's words about bounty hunters and men
who would pay dearly to get their hands on
the Cheyenne Wells money.

When he hit the Arkansas River a few
miles east of Pueblo he followed the easterly
flow to Rocky Ford which he reached late
one evening. The next day he replenished
his supplies and shortly before noon headed
for the bank. He smiled to himself when he

recognised the sheriff who had captured him and saw him lean on the rail, his rifle held in the crook of his arm as he watched him approach the bank. The lawman was puzzled by the fact that Brady should be going to that particular building but what surprised him more was the fact that Brady was not wearing a gun-belt.

Vance went straight to the manager's office and gave that official the surprise of his life when he walked in.

'Don't look so shocked,' grinned Vance. 'I thought you'd be pleased to see me, especially as I've come to close my account. Unless you've closed it already,' he added, making sure his meaning was not lost on the bank manager.

'Your money's still safe,' came the terse reply.

'Good,' said Brady. 'I'll take the lot.'

'But I can't do that right away,' protested the manager. 'There'll be twenty-five thousand dollars to your name and if I issue that it will leave us short for other transactions.'

'You'll git round those all right,' said Vance. 'I want the lot now, otherwise...'

The bank manager did not let him finish his threat. 'Very well, I'll arrange it,' he snapped irritably. He rose from his chair and stormed out of his office to return a few moments later with the money. He shoved it angrily at Brady and breathed a sigh of relief when the ex-bank robber left his office.

Vance returned to the hotel where he remained for the rest of the day. Figuring that the sheriff would be prepared to follow him when he left town, hoping to be lead to the Cheyenne Wells money, Vance reckoned he would have a better chance of outwitting any followers at night.

Darkness covered Rocky Ford when Brady gathered his belongings and hurried along the corridor to a window which led on to a wooden stairway acting as a fire-escape. He moved swiftly but silently down the steps to the back of the hotel, but had gone only a few yards when he realised someone was following him. He cursed to himself; the sheriff had taken all precautions!

Two blocks along Vance turned into a side street alongside the store. Once round the corner he dropped his saddle-bags and crouched close to the corner of the build-ings. The footsteps slowed and Vance knew the man was approaching the corner with care. Brady stooped down, picked up two stones and threw them along the street. The ruse worked; the man, thinking Vance was still hurrying through the town, increased his pace, turned the corner quickly and was on top of Brady before he realised it. As soon as the figure appeared Vance leaped forward, driving his fist into the man's face. The lawman staggered backwards and before he could recover Brady was at him again. The blow caught him squarely on the jaw, spread-eagling him in the dust. Vance quickly secured the man's legs and hands with his own belt and tied the neckerchief over his mouth. Gathering his things together Brady hurried to the main street which he entered cautiously. He noticed the sheriff sitting outside his office watching the hotel, so, keeping to the shadows, he made his way to the livery stable and was soon riding quietly out of town.

Once clear of Rocky Ford he put his horse into a fast trot and rode far into the night before he decided to camp.

During the next two days he moved steadily southwards, climbing through the mountainous country to the Goodnight-Loving trail over Raton Pass into New Mexico. He continued his progress southwards and two days later rode into the small town of Wagon Mound.

Dominated by the surrounding mountains

Wagon Mound showed every sign of being a mining town which had enjoyed only a moderate boom and was now on the decline. It boasted two stores, a stage office, one hotel and one saloon. Other buildings stood empty and Vance reckoned that unless another strike was made Wagon Mound would soon be a ghost town.

He pulled up outside the hotel and strolled inside.

'I'd like a room for a few days,' he said after waking up the clerk whom he found dozing in a chair behind his desk.

'You can have one for as long as you like,' replied the clerk eyeing Vance up and down. 'Not often we get anyone of your type wanting to stay here,' he added.

'Times bad?' asked Vance.

'Well, we've seen better but we still get plenty of miners and prospectors coming in here. There are two mines operating about ten miles from here; nothing big, mind you, but sufficient to keep men interested. The saloon does moderately well but even that has seen bigger crowds thronging the bar and the tables.'

Vance was pleased to find the clerk talkative. 'It's my first time down this way,' he said. 'I think you might be able to help me.'

'Do my best,' replied the clerk brightly.

'I'm looking for someone by the name of Della Jenkins,' said Vance.

The clerk rubbed his chin thoughtfully. 'The name doesn't ring a bell immediately,' he said. 'Do you know anything about her?'

'She came from Greely up in Colorado,' said Brady. 'She'd be about twenty-three now and was last heard of about three years ago and the letter came from this town.'

The clerk smiled. 'Thet was when we were enjoying better times,' he said. 'A lot of people came here then, most passed on; she could have been one of those. Only people by the name of Della living here now are Mrs Crayston and Mrs Tessler, but they're too old to be the girl you're referring to.'

Brady looked disappointed. 'Thanks,' he said. 'If you can think of anything which may help let me know. I'll make a few enquiries about town.'

He went upstairs to his room and after freshening up he took his horse to the livery stable and then sought out the doctor, but again he drew a blank; the name of Della Jenkins meant nothing to him.

Vance strolled along the sidewalk trying to figure out his next move. He had been hopeful when he had ridden in to Wagon Mound

63

but now in a very short space of time his hopes had been dashed. He had looked forward to meeting Ace's wife and he badly wanted to help her but realised that as she had not stopped long in Wagon Mound her whereabouts would be extremely hard to find.

Vance found himself outside the saloon and pushing open the batwings he walked over to the bar. When he had obtained his beer he went to a table which gave him a commanding view of the room. There were about thirty people, mostly miners, sitting at the tables and six men stood at the long counter. Vance's eyes rested on a table at the far end of the saloon where a young woman sat by herself idly toying with a deck of cards. Her face was pale and even from this distance Vance detected a sadness in her eyes. He guessed she looked older than she really was and yet there was a certain beauty about her, an attractiveness which caught Vance's attention.

She appeared to be better dressed than the other saloon girls; her dark green satin frock came to her feet and accentuated the curves of her body. The dress was topless and revealed smooth shoulders. The young woman looked up and met Vance's gaze. A smile flicked her lips and an inviting twinkle came into her eye. Vance knew that this must have been done hundreds of times to get men to play that deck of cards, but in spite of this he pushed himself to his feet and strolled slowly to her table.

''Evenin', miss,' drawled Vance as he sat down on the chair opposite to her and removed his sombrero.

'Hello, cowboy,' greeted the girl with a smile which showed a row of even white teeth. 'We don't get many of you down this way now.'

'Buy you a drink?' asked Vance.

'Thanks,' said the girl. 'Charlie will know what to bring.' Vance called to the barman who brought the drinks. 'Staying in town long?' she asked.

'Thet depends, miss,' replied Vance.

'Call me Laura, everybody does,' she said.

Vance smiled. 'Vance Brady,' he answered, offering his name in exchange.

The girl visibly stiffened, the smile vanished and a mixture of astonishment and hate flashed in her eyes. 'Vance Brady,' she hissed in a long drawn-out whisper. Her hands were clenched so tight that her knuckles showed white. Vance was surprised and taken aback at the effect his name had on her. He looked at her questioningly seeking some answer with his eyes.

'For years I've wanted to meet you; for years I've hoped that prison would break you and now, here you are, in front of me, fit and healthy as if nothing had happened and Ace lying cold all this time because he had to ride to Cheyenne Walls with you.' Laura spat each word slowly and deliberately from her lips, putting a feeling of hate into each one as if trying to burn them forever into Vance's heart.

Brady stared in amazement at her. He was so surprised that he could not find a word to say.

Laura pushed herself from her chair, drawing herself to her full height. She looked down contemptuously at Vance. 'Because of Ace's loyalty to you I came to this, a saloon woman; it was entertain men or starve. Take a good look, Mister Brady, I'm only twenty-three and every night in the mirror I look for the lost years. I was beginning to forget the past; eighteen months ago, Mel Walker took over this saloon and me with it; I became a one-man woman to run this place for him. Now you show up and remind me of...' A falter came into her voice. Vance looked up and saw tears being held back forcibly.

He seized the opportunity. 'Sit down, please, sit down and let me explain, Della; you must be Della in spite of the name you use now,' he said quietly. 'I did not come to hurt you.'

His eyes were soft and full of pity. He reached out and took hold of her wrist. Slowly she sat down and stared at him. 'Well, Mister Brady, I'm listening,' she said haughtily.

'When Ace came to me that night I didn't know he was married, he never told me,' explained Vance. 'If I had I would never have gone through with the plan. I only learned about you when I came out of jail. The old friend who told me also informed me that he saw Ace just before he joined me and he had told him it was to be his last robbery.'

'If he had told me what he really was I would still have married him, but I would never have let him go,' said Della bitterly. 'I know I could have changed him.'

'I'm sure you could,' said Vance. 'Don't blame Ace for what happened to you. From what I hear your parents must bear that.'

'What do you know of them?' asked Della sharply.

Brady went on to tell her how he had seen

Fay Carlyle and what she had told him.

'Poor Fay,' remarked Della. 'Her father wouldn't…' She left the sentence unfinished and shrugged her shoulders. 'But what does it matter now?'

'I did a great deal of thinking in prison,' said Vance. 'I swore that I would find the dependents of Ace and the young cowboy who was with us and that they should have a fair share of the money.' Della looked up sharply and stared at Vance. 'There is a tidy sum due to you, Della, it could take you out of this place back to the life you knew.'

'Do you think that money can change me from the life I now know; aren't the marks of that on me for ever?' remarked Della bitterly. 'Oh, I'm not turning down your offer, Mister Brady, but that sweet girl of eighteen who married Ace Jenkins has gone for ever.'

Vance was at a loss to know what to say. He fought to find words adequate enough to express his feelings but could not. 'I'm glad I've found you, Della, and I will do all I can to help. I cannot tell you how much…'

He was interrupted when a miner came up to the table. 'I'd like to try my luck,' he said indicating the cards.

'We're busy,' rapped Vance.

The miner stiffened. He looked belligerently at the cowboy.

'I'm sorry, Mister Brady, we'll have to talk later,' put in Della quickly, sensing the tenseness of the moment. 'This is what I'm here for and this man is a customer.' Words of protestation sprung to Vance's lips but were stopped as Della went on. 'Please come back this evening, I'd like to think things over.'

Vance nodded, picked up his sombrero and left the table.

Throughout the next half hour Della's mind did not concentrate on the cards but kept turning to the interview with Vance Brady. As soon as the miner had had enough she called to one of the girls to take over the table and hurried from the saloon along a passage to a door at the far end. She entered a large well-furnished room one corner of which was occupied by a large mahogany desk. As soon as she walked in a man rose from his chair behind the desk and came to meet her. He was immaculately dressed in a grey frock coat and matching trousers which were topped by a fancy embroidered waistcoat covering a white silk shirt. His long face was thinnish and tended to be on the pale side. The sleek black hair was brushed back and a thin moustache was obviously well-cared for.

'Hello, Della,' his dark eyes flashed a smile and his lips parted to show a row of white even teeth. He took her by the shoulders and kissed her. She was not eager in her return and as she turned away Mel looked questioningly at her. 'Something wrong?' he asked.

She shrugged her shoulders. 'Not really,' she replied. 'I've just had a bit of a shock; something from the past came up again.'

Walker was beside her quickly. His slim hands gripped her firmly by the shoulders and he looked deep into her eyes. 'I told you to forget all that,' he said smoothly. 'It's just you and I now. If anyone has thrown it up at you to hurt you I'll deal with them.' There was a sharpness in his voice which bore ill for anyone who troubled Della.

'It wasn't like that really,' answered Della. She paused thoughtfully then smiled as if shaking off the mood in which she had entered the room. 'I suppose I should be pleased and be coming in here to tell you the good news.

Mel Walker was curious but he did not rush her; he knew she would enlighten him in her own time. He crossed the room to a large mahogany sideboard and poured out two drinks. He took a glass to Della, who had sat down in an easy chair, and waited for her to continue her story. Della sipped at the drink before telling Mel of her encounter with Vance.

'The shock of seeing this man made me bitter at first,' she concluded, 'but I see it is no use bringing up the past again.' She smiled and suddenly brightened. 'Oh, Mel, with this money we can get out of Wagon Mound and buy the big place we've always dreamed about, bringing in hundreds of customers instead of the handful we get in here,' she said enthusiastically.

Mel had listened intently to everything she had said. His cool, calculating brain was working fast and already big schemes were growing before his eyes.

'We could,' he said thoughtfully as he selected a cigar from a box on his desk. He lit it carefully, blew a long cloud of smoke into the air and looked hard at Della.

'How would you like to play for bigger stakes?' he asked.

'What do you mean?' asked Della.

'I reckon Brady will offer you Ace's share of that raid,' he said. 'Now there'll be a lot more money than that and I figure if we play the thing carefully we can lay our hands on the lot.'

'What!' gasped Della. 'I'm willing to settle for what he offers, it will be enough. Don't try and meddle with Vance Brady, Mel. I don't want to lose you.'

'You won't,' answered Mel.

'But why bother?' asked Della. 'And even so, how are we going to find out where the money is?'

Walker smiled. 'How? I don't know yet. That depends on how much you can learn from Brady when he comes tonight. Why? Because I think you are entitled to more than Ace's share. Look what happened to you after Ace was killed.' Mel warmed to his subject; he pressed his ideas hard and his persuasive tongue soon made Della think he was right. 'If Brady hadn't saved the sheriff your husband would still be alive and from what you've told me you would have persuaded him to go straight. You wouldn't have fallen to the degrading life you had to lead at times. All this was due to Brady saving a lawman's life, saved a life at the expense of a man supposed to be his best friend. I reckon Brady owes you a lot more than Ace's share; he owes you for all those times you crawled in the gutter until I came to Wagon Mound and saw you. That's the only reason I'm grateful for what Brady did; if he hadn't I wouldn't have had you.' Della stared thoughtfully in front of her all the time that Mel was speaking. An anger and hate slowly smouldered in her eyes as she saw things his way. 'You deserve more,' he went on, 'and with it we can really go big: St Louis, New York, San Francisco, even Europe, anywhere you like, Della, the world could be yours. We'll build the biggest saloon and gambling house on the Pacific Coast and it will be yours and people will flock to Della's to see the beautiful owner, the Queen of the Pacific. What about it, Della?'

She did not speak for a few minutes but still stared straight ahead. Her thoughts had raced as Mel persuaded, she conjured up everything that lay before her with the sort of wealth Mel was aiming at. Slowly she looked up at Mel who puffed his cigar and watched her carefully through the curling smoke.

'Very well, Mel, we'll do it.' Her voice was soft and quiet but Walker knew that with this tone went a determination second to none. 'What do you want me to do?'

Mel smiled and dropped on one knee beside the chair on which Della was sitting.

He gripped her arm tightly. 'Good girl,' he said eagerly. 'There's nothing we can't do. When Brady comes tonight play along with him, tell him you'd like the money in cash and quick, find out where he has it if possible, what his intentions are and anything else which might be of value to us.' He stood up, a triumphant smile on his face. 'One thing, though, don't introduce him to me.'

'Why not?' asked Della.

'It might prove useful if I'm not known.'

Della pushed herself from the chair and turned to Mel. 'Just as you say, Mel. You can be certain that Vance Brady will see my womanly charms.' She slid her hands slowly up the lapels of Mel's coat and pressed her body close to his. As her hands slid round his collar she reached forward to kiss him full on the lips.

There were more people in the saloon when Vance Brady entered it that same evening. Vance paused inside the batwings and surveyed the room. Catching sight of Della he walked slowly towards her. She watched him carefully as he approached and smiled a warm welcome as he removed his sombrero to greet her. He bought her a drink and when they had finished it she led him to her room at the back of the saloon.

'Thought it would be quieter to talk here,' she said as she poured him another drink. 'I'm sorry for the way I spoke this afternoon, but it was a shock when you told me you were Vance Brady.'

'I'm sorry about that,' replied Vance, 'but in a way it served a purpose; it has saved me checking up on you. From the way you reacted I knew you were Della Jenkins in spite of the fact that you're known here as Laura.'

Della smiled. 'Well, I'm glad some good came of it,' she said. 'And I hope you won't hold my remarks against me.'

'Certainly not, Della,' smiled Vance. 'I'm only too pleased I have found you and part of the plans I formulated in prison have been fulfilled.'

'What do you mean by part?' asked Della curiously.

'Ace brought a young cowboy with him,' explained Vance. 'You may remember he was killed too. Well, I want to find his widow and see that you are both well provided for.'

'You are very generous,' said Della smoothly. 'That means the money is to be split three ways?'

'I'm not sure about that,' replied Vance, 'but I will guarantee not less than twenty thousand dollars.'

Della stared wide-eyed at Vance. A little gasp escaped her lips. 'Then I can get out of this place tomorrow!' she said, excitement in her eyes.

'It is not quite as simple as that,' said Vance. 'I want to find this other person first. If I fail you'll maybe get more, apart from which I haven't the money with me. You'll just have to be a little patient, Della, but now that I've found you so quickly I'll get on my way tomorrow.' Vance rose to his feet. 'Don't worry if I'm away some time for I'll not forget you. Ace was my best friend and I feel I'll be paying a debt this way.'

Della tried to persuade Vance to stay longer hoping that she would get more information from him, but Vance insisted on leaving. As the door closed behind him Della's eyes stared coldly after him.

'Maybe, sixty thousand dollars!' she whispered to herself. 'What Mel and I could do with that when you have been taken care of!'

She hurried from her room and sought out Mel Walker, telling him of Brady's plans.

Mel smiled. 'That's a great deal of money to play for,' he said, 'and honey, I think I'd better keep an eye on this personally. Tomorrow I'll take Butch Nolan with me and your clever Mister Brady will have two shadows on his trail until he leads us to that cash!'

When Vance Brady rode down the main street of Wagon Mound the following morning two men watched him from the doorway of a saloon. Everything had been prepared early and when Brady reached the edge of town Mel Walker and his sidekick swung into the saddles and turned their horses to follow.

Vance Brady had only the slenderest of clues to go on; Tom Corby had been a drover from Texas and Texas was a big stretch of country to search.

Chapter Five

Jed Owen, Sheriff of Plainview, strolled out of his office and paused on the sidewalk. He glanced along the main street then lowered his short, stocky frame into a chair beside the door. The afternoon was hot and all was normal in the small Texas town. Two cowboys greeted him as they strolled past. He looked after them, then when his gaze passed beyond them, he frowned on seeing Wes Carter lounging in a chair outside the hotel.

Wes Carter, dark, swarthy, had been hanging around Plainview for the past two weeks and Jed did not like him. He had given no trouble but the sheriff recognised him as a bounty hunter and Jed had no time for men who lived off the misfortune of their fellow men.

He distrusted bounty hunters and the lengths they would go to earn the price on a man's head. He wondered why Carter should choose to stay in Plainview but he could not tell him to move on; he had not disturbed the peace.

Jed glanced at a horseman who had appeared at one end of the town and was riding slowly along the main street. Suddenly he stiffened, his eyes widening with surprise.

'Vance Brady!' he gasped to himself. His thoughts raced. Was this the reason why Carter was in town? Had he known Brady was heading for Plainview? Even if he hadn't Jed realised there could be trouble brewing. He watched Carter carefully. So far the bounty hunter showed no sign of having seen Brady. Owen pushed himself out of the chair and moved forward to lean on the rail. The horseman started to swing across the street towards the hotel and as he did so the sheriff saw Carter sit upright in his chair and stare in the direction of Brady. Jed felt a coldness sweep over him; Carter had recognised Brady and Brady had a price on his head in three states!

As Vance Brady pulled to a halt in front of the hotel and swung from the saddle Wes Carter climbed out of his chair and moved to the top of the two steps which led from the dusty road on to the sidewalk. He was eyeing Brady carefully and when Vance moved to mount the sidewalk he stepped in front of him. Vance checked his step and made to go round the man in his way but Carter stepped in his path again. Brady stopped and looked up at the man who prevented him from going to the hotel. He saw a dark man with a thin moustache whose face was split by a leering smile of self-satisfaction. Vance's gaze swept across the man whose clothes showed distinct signs of wear. His boots were dusty and his sombrero stained but the thing which really caught Vance's eye was the smooth butt of the Colt which hung in a worn holster. Vance knew he was confronted by a man used to drawing that gun.

'Howdy, Brady,' grinned Carter. 'I've been hangin' around this dump fer two weeks trying to decide which trail to hit, mighty glad I spent so long now thet you've obligingly ridden in peaceful like.'

Vance eyed the stranger shrewdly, pursing his lips thoughtfully.

'I'm afraid I haven't had the pleasure before,' replied Vance coolly.

Carter laughed. 'I'll say you haven't,' he said. 'If you hed you wouldn't be here now.' He paused; the smile slowly vanished from his face and he stared hard at Brady. 'I'm Wes Carter an' I guess you'd better git to know me 'cos you're goin' to see a lot of me whilst we head north.'

'I aren't goin' anywhere,' replied Vance. His voice was cold and full of menace. 'I'm stayin' right here.'

'Thet's what you think,' answered Carter. 'There's two thousand dollars on your head in Wyoming, Dakota and Missouri an' I figure on collectin' one of those rewards.' As he spoke Carter had drawn his Colt and held it casually pointing at Brady. 'I see you don't wear a gun now,' went on the bounty hunter. 'Thet's mighty thoughtful of you; it cuts out any unpleasantness which might hev arisen.'

Vance realised he was in a hopeless position at the moment but he had no intention of letting this bounty hunter spoil his plans. He was in Texas where he was a free man and he was not going to be taken out of it at the point of a gun.

'I guess it will be jest like goin' home fer you, seein' you've jest come out of the pen,' said Carter smoothly. He saw Brady stiffen under the taunt and, being a man who liked to see others squirm under his power, he went on. 'They let you out a few months early. Reckon you must hev been a good little boy, wal, if you behave yourself again may be you'll git another remission. All right, let's go! There's no time like the present.'

He motioned with his gun and without a word Vance turned slowly and stepped towards his horse.

He untied the reins from the hitching rail and climbed into the saddle. He held the horse steady whilst Carter circled him to his own horse. As he swung upwards to the animal's back his gun wavered. Vance seized the opportunity. He lashed upwards with his foot sending the gun flying from Carter's grasp. Almost in the same movement he flung himself at Carter dragging him to the ground. As they hit the hard earth Brady's grip on Carter broke and both men twisted, scrambling to their feet. A black look of anger and hate darkened Carter's face as he lunged at Brady. The momentum carried both men crashing into Carter's horse, sending the animal stomping a few paces down the street. The two men hit the ground with a thud and an evil grin of triumph crossed Carter's face when he found himself on top of Brady. His fist crashed hard against Vance's cheek but before another blow could be struck Brady brought his knees upwards and at the same time jerked at Carter's arms, sending him flying over his head. The breath was driven from Carter's body by the throw and by the time Brady had jumped to his feet and leaped towards him Carter had only scrambled to his knees. Vance hit him viciously under the chin, jerking his head backwards and tumbling him once more into the dust.

Brady moved forward, his eyes glinting viciously. Sheriff Owen, who had heard and watched the whole proceedings carefully, saw the fiery look and realised that here was a man who was prepared to defend his freedom almost at all costs. The sheriff sprang into action and jumped from the sidewalk in front of Vance as he moved towards the bounty hunter who, shaking his head, was struggling to get up. Jed pushed Vance away.

'Hold off!' he snapped.

Vance moved forward again to try to pass the sheriff but he found himself up against the hard muzzle of the Colt which Jed had drawn swiftly. It was then that Vance noticed the tin-star pinned to the brown shirt of the man in front of him. It seemed to jerk Vance up with a jolt and the vicious gleam in his eyes slowly faded. Jed Owen noticed it and stepped to one side so that he had both men covered by his gun. Carter pushed himself shakily to his feet and stood with legs astride glaring sullenly at both Vance and the lawman.

'Thet's enough,' rapped the sheriff. 'This town is peaceful an' it's goin' to stay thet way as long as I'm the sheriff.'

'It won't as long as he's here,' hissed Carter.

'I'll see it does,' snapped Jed.

'Don't you know who this is?' gasped Carter almost incredulously.

'Vance Brady,' replied the sheriff coldly.

'You don't seem concerned,' said Carter with surprise. 'He's a notorious bank robber wanted in three states.'

'But not in Texas,' pointed out Jed firmly.

'As long as he behaves himself here then thet's all I ask, an' so far he's done nothin' wrong.'

'You're runnin' a risk with the town's money, keepin' Brady around,' replied Carter glancing at the people, who had gathered around when the first started, but there was no backing from them; they respected the judgment of their sheriff. 'I'd save you a lot of trouble if I took him to Wyoming.'

'I reckon the best way to save Plainview any trouble is fer you to ride out of here now,' rapped Jed. 'I don't like bounty hunters an' still less do I like them hangin' around my town.' Carter started to protest but the sheriff cut him short. 'Move!' he snapped. He stepped forward menacingly. Carter glared angrily at the sheriff, picked up his dust-covered sombrero and turned to his horse.

The group of people watched the bounty hunter climb into the saddle. He turned the animal away from the rail then stopped and looked down at the sheriff and Vance Brady.

'I'll be back,' he hissed and kicked his horse into a gallop, heading northwards along the main street.

As the dust rose behind the bounty hunter the townspeople of Plainview returned to their everyday business discussing the appearance of Vance Brady.

Jed Owen turned to Brady. 'I believe you were goin' into the hotel,' he said. 'When you've booked in an' got cleaned up come along to my office.'

Brady nodded and watched the sheriff as he walked away. He judged the lawman to be about thirty-five and knew from what had happened that he was a tough man who would stand no nonsense but who would be fair and prepared to hear both sides of a story and judge accordingly. Vance walked slowly into the hotel and, after booking a room and taking a bath, he put on fresh clothes and made his way to the sheriff's office.

Sheriff Owen was sitting behind his desk when Vance opened the door and stepped into the office. He saw a man neatly turned out in a clean white shirt and black trousers tucked neatly into the top of shining black calf-length boots. Jed indicated a chair to the newcomer.

'Thanks,' said Vance, 'and thanks for what you did out there. It puzzles me why you should support me, a man who has been on the wrong side of the law.'

Jed looked hard at Vance before he spoke.

'Wal, fer one thing bounty hunters are a race apart an' not generally liked. Carter's been hangin' around town fer a couple of weeks; it's a pity he hadn't moved on before you got here. I don't hold with bounty hunters an' as far as I'm concerned you've done nothin' wrong here, it was Carter who started the trouble.'

'I reckon he may come back,' said Vance thoughtfully.

'If he does he'd better walk carefully, however, you'd better look out fer yourself if you figure on stayin' around here long.'

Brady ignored this hint for information and eyed the sheriff wryly. 'I hev a feelin' thet it wasn't jest because he was a bounty hunter thet you took the course you did.'

The sheriff smiled. 'Guess you're right,' he said. 'When Vance Brady rides into town after serving a prison sentence an' he's not wearin' a gun then somethin' has changed him. Oh, I know you've never killed a lawman, an' thet you've only shot in self-defence, but the fact that your reputation for a lightning fast draw was well known prevented many men from tackling you. Wearing a gun was a means of defence in itself for you. In fact if you'd been wearin' one I doubt if Carter would hev tackled you so openly.' Jed paused.

'What's this leadin' up to, Sheriff?' asked Vance.

'Wal, I figured it this way,' went on Jed. 'Vance Brady, without a gun, in a territory in which he has never operated, is not lookin' fer trouble; maybe prison changed him, maybe he wants to change his ways, after all he's an intelligent man, not a common everyday bank robber, so I figured if I was right he deserved a chance; and after all I suppose in some ways I am in his debt.'

Brady looked at the sheriff curiously, a surprised, puzzled expression on his face.

'You, in my debt?' he asked.

Jed smiled. 'I'd better introduce myself,' he said. 'Jed Owen.' He paused but, seeing that the name had not registered with Brady he went on. 'You saved my brother's life after the raid on the bank at Cheyenne Wells. He was the sheriff an' I figure if you hadn't interfered when thet young cowboy went fer his gun you'd hev all got clean away.'

Vance smiled. 'Maybe we would,' he said, 'but we'd hev had a price on our heads fer murder an' would hev swung for it some day. I've often reproached myself for the deaths of my two buddies. However, thet's all behind me an' you don't owe me a thing.'

'Wal, I figure I do,' drawled Jed, 'but thet won't influence my upholding the law if you step out of line.'

'I wouldn't expect it to,' answered Brady. 'An' I hope you won't hev to come after me. You were right about the gun an' prison. Thet was my first taste of it an' I don't want to be shut up again. I love the open spaces an' I am determined to go straight so thet I don't end up behind bars again. Thet's why I came this way an' thet's why I was determined to fight Carter.'

'Then wear a gun,' said the sheriff. 'I know you won't use it unless forced to, an' as I said, the fact that you wear one will prove a certain insurance against anyone tryin' to take you back north.'

Vance shook his head. 'I reckon they'd still come lookin' fer me an' some day a man who was faster than me would come along. If I don't wear one maybe people will git used to the idea that Vance Brady has settled down an' will leave me alone.'

'You could be right,' said the sheriff, 'but there will always be men to be tempted by the bounty.'

'If they know where I am,' answered Vance. 'It was just my bad luck thet Carter should be here.' He paused thoughtfully.

'Look here, Sheriff,' he went on, 'I am in Texas for another purpose but that can wait; I like the look of the country around here an' I would like to buy a small spread not too far from town; do you know a likely place?'

The sheriff looked thoughtful for a few moments. 'There are a few sections of land around here but I figure there might be a good chance of gettin' the Running J. It is a fair-sized spread but not too big; reckon it might just suit you. Gil Rogers was thrown from his horse and killed a month ago, his widow can't really make up her mind whether to try to carry on or sell up an' go back to St Louis to her folks. A good price might persuade her to make up her mind.'

'Tell her to name her price an' I'll meet it,' said Vance enthusiastically.

'I'll hev a word with her,' replied Jed, 'but I'll not close the deal, you'll hev to see the place first.'

'I'm sure it will be all right if you say so, but I'll hev a look at it if you'd rather I did,' agreed Brady.

'Good,' said Jed. 'Drop in here tomorrow afternoon, I might hev more news fer you by then.'

Brady pushed himself to his feet, thanked the sheriff and strolled out of the office to take a look at Plainview.

Chapter Six

Wes Carter left Plainview at a steady trot. His face was black with anger and annoyance; he smarted under the fact that Brady had outwitted and out-fought him and that the sheriff had ordered him out of town, showing him up in front of the town folk. His thoughts raced, wondering what Vance Brady was doing in Plainview, and planning how he could get him to the Wyoming authorities in order to collect that enticing reward money. The thought of that made Carter all the more determined, and of one thing he was certain, he would have to keep an eye on Brady's movements.

About three miles north of town Wes left the trail and circled back toward Plainview. He approached from the west and was able to slip unseen through the side-streets and alleys to the back of the saloon. He slid from the saddle, secured his horse and, finding the back door of the saloon open, he stepped inside the building. A flight of stairs led upwards from the narrow passage. Wes mounted them quickly and in a few moments was tapping lightly on the third door along the corridor. Receiving no reply, Wes turned the knob and, finding the door unlocked, walked into the room, closing the door behind him. He smiled to himself as he looked round the room which bore the obvious signs of a feminine occupant. Wes flopped into an armchair, stretched his legs in front of him and waited.

Twenty minutes passed before footsteps tripped along the corridor and a young woman of about twenty-four entered the room. She wore a vivid red frock which came just below her knees revealing shapely legs. Her shoulders and arms were bare and her hair was piled high on her head. She stepped forward towards the dressing-table then jumped with startled surprise when she realised Wes Carter was sitting in the chair.

'Wes, what are you doing in here?' she snapped irritably, her eyes blazing with annoyance at the fact that Carter had been so presumptuous as to walk into her room to wait for her.

'Came to see you, honey.' He flashed a smile at the girl as she pouted.

She moved towards the dressing-table and Wes grabbed her wrist, pulled her down on to his knee, encircled her with his free arm and pulled her close to him to kiss her passionately full on her lips. For a brief moment the girl resisted, then relaxed, slid her arm round his neck and returned his kiss. When their lips parted she pushed herself from his knee and as she straightened her dress she glanced shrewdly at Wes.

'Now tell me what you really came for,' she said. 'I heard you'd been kicked out of town by the sheriff.'

Wes stiffened in his chair and his eyes narrowed as her words recalled his failure.

'No one pushes me around an' gits away with it,' he snapped.

'Then you've returned to get your revenge?' asked the girl.

'On the sheriff – indirectly, Mavis,' replied Wes. 'He stopped me takin' Vance Brady; there's a price on his head in Wyoming an' I mean to hev it. I'll git him yet in spite of Sheriff Jed Owen.'

'But why come to me?' asked Mavis.

'I'm gettin' out of town fer a couple of days,' explained Carter. 'Make them think

I've cleared. I want you to get to know all you can about Brady's movements.' He looked for agreement from the girl but she did not reply immediately. 'There's money in this, Mavis, big money,' went on Carter excitedly to press his case. 'When we get it we'll get married an' get you away from Plainview.'

Mavis tapped her lips thoughtfully as she looked at Wes.

'Do you know how long Brady's stopping in town?' she asked.

Wes shook his head. 'I hadn't time to find that out,' he replied testily.

'It's no good you disappearing for a couple of days if Brady is moving on tomorrow,' pointed out Mavis.

'Guess not,' agreed Wes. 'I didn't think of that; I presumed he'd be stayin' here for a while.'

Mavis looked at Wes with disgust. 'Thet's the trouble with you,' she said irritably, 'you may be handy with a gun but you don't think deep enough.' She picked up her coat and swung it round her shoulders. 'Stay here, Wes, I'll see what I can find out.'

'Good girl,' grinned Wes and slapped her thigh as she passed him, 'we'll make a great team.'

Mavis did not reply but swung out of the room and hurried down the back stairs. Once outside she made her way to the main street, crossed the dusty roadway to the livery stable three blocks away. As she turned through the double doors Ben Porter glanced up from the stall which he was cleaning. The old man, who still fancied himself with the ladies, was so surprised to see Mavis Cameron coming into the livery stable that he dropped his brush. He smoothed his moustache and hurried to meet her as fast as his bow-legs would carry him.

'Howdy, Mavis,' he greeted with a chuckle. 'Couldn't you wait for me to come to the saloon tonight?'

Mavis smiled back at him. 'It's always a pleasure to see you, Ben,' she replied smoothly as she linked her arm through his. 'I hope you'll be there tonight.'

The old man chuckled. 'Sure will, Mavis, sure will.'

'Then maybe you can help me,' said the girl. 'A stranger rode into town today; has he stabled his horse here?'

'Sure has, Mavis,' replied Ben, 'an' a mighty fine animal he was ridin', thet's it over there.' He indicated a horse half-way along the stable, but Mavis was not interested in it.

'Did he say if he was staying long?' she asked.

Ben eyed her suspiciously. 'Now you aren't takin' a fancy to him, are you?' he grunted.

Mavis laughed. 'Of course not, Ben, so you needn't be jealous. One of the girls at the Golden Cage thought she knew him from way back an' I said I'd find out.'

Ben grinned sheepishly. 'I wasn't gettin' jealous,' he said. 'He might be here some time, didn't say but he remarked about likin' the country around here.'

Mavis nodded thoughtfully. 'Thanks, Ben,' she said. 'See you later.' She unlinked her arm and started towards the door.

Ben looked after her curiously then called out, 'Mavis.' The girl stopped and turned to face him. 'Surely the other girl would hev recognised Vance Brady if she'd known him before?'

Mavis suddenly realised she had nearly made a slip in her approach to Ben Porter. She thought fast. 'Then it can't hev been the man she thought,' Mavis said. 'You're sure it was Vance Brady – the notorious bank robber, you mean?'

'Yeah,' answered Ben, 'thet's jest who I mean. I'm not mistaken, I saw him up in

Wyoming an' I never fergit a face.'

Mavis nodded; thanked Ben again and left the stable. She hurried back to the Golden Cage and found Wes Carter still sitting in the chair as she had left him.

'Wal?' he drawled when Mavis entered the room.

'I reckon he could be staying a few days,' replied Mavis and went on to relate what Ben had told her.

'Good,' said Wes when she had finished. 'I'll disappear until the day after tomorrow, I'll come in mid-afternoon; see what you can find out by then.' Carter pushed himself to his feet. He put his hands on Mavis' shoulders and looked down into her dark brown eyes. 'You're a smart girl, honey, an' you an' me will hit it rich at the expense of clever Mister Brady.' He bent forward and kissed her upturned face on the lips which were offered to him. As they parted he whispered, 'This is our big chance.' He stepped past her and left her room.

Once outside he untied his horse, swung into the saddle and left town quickly, circling until he joined the north road five miles out of Plainview. He rode at a brisk pace well satisfied with the way things were taking a turn for him. It was a hot day and by the time Wes Carter reached Tulia, where he intended to stay, he was ready to slake his thirst. He pulled up in front of the saloon and after hitching his horse to the rail he pushed open the batwings and walked to the long mahogany counter. He ordered a beer and as soon as it was put in front of him he drained the glass and ordered another. Wes paid for the two drinks when the second one was brought and, then leaning his elbows on the counter, proceeded to drink his beer slowly whilst observing the occupants of the saloon through the long mirror on the wall behind the counter.

Ten minutes passed before Wes heard the batwings squeak and saw two dust-covered, travel-stained men approaching the bar. Wes studied them through the mirror as they picked their way between the tables. One of them was neatly turned out in a brown shirt and fawn coloured trousers, the legs of which came over the tops of his black boots. A black string tie was fastened around his neck and his head was covered by a grey, wide-brimmed, flat-crowned sombrero. His companion, who was obviously his side-kick, wore a dark blue shirt and blue jeans tucked into the top of black boots. The brim of his sombrero was well curled and a frayed neckerchief was tied loosely at his throat. Both men wore Colts strapped to their right legs.

Wes cast the men a casual glance as they reached the bar close to him and called for some drinks. Wes continued to watch the men through the mirror. The man with the string-tie, whose features were sharp with a certain paleness about them, had a thin well-trimmed moustache which seemed to give a certain charm to him. Wes was curious about him for he did not seem to be a man who would be found far from a town. His eyes seemed to be taking in everything and Wes judged him to be shrewd, a man who would play for big stakes in a careful methodical manner and yet be prepared to take a risk if necessary. Carter turned his attention to the other man and saw he was rough and rugged with a nose which showed the obvious sign of having been broken. His fingers were broad and gnarled in marked contrast to those of his moustached companion which were smooth and supple with well-trimmed finger-nails. Wes judged them to be a gambler with a rough, tough sidekick to fight the dirty side of his battles.

They called for another drink and when the barman brought their beer the moustached man detained him.

'We are trying to catch up with a friend of ours,' he said. 'We know he was heading south but lost his trail yesterday; we wondered if you have had any strangers in here today.'

'There hev been three men unknown to me in here today,' he replied, then dropped his voice a little. 'One of them there,' he added, nodding in the direction of Wes.

'Not him,' came the reply. 'What about the other two?'

'Left shortly before noon,' answered the barman.

'Together?'

'No,' the barman replied.

'The man we are looking for is tall, well-built, be about twenty-eight, rather good-looking in a rugged sort of way, his eyes are rather striking – deep blue.'

The barman shook his head. 'Sorry,' he said. 'Your description doesn't fit. One of these was a Mexican an' the other short and dark and I'd hardly call him handsome.' He moved away to serve another customer and the two men took their beer to a table and sat down.

Wes watched them for a moment then picked up his glass and strolled casually to the same table. The two men looked up curiously when he stopped in front of them.

'Mind if I sit down,' drawled Wes casually. 'I think I might hev the information you require.'

The man with the moustache regarded Wes shrewdly and then indicated a vacant chair. Wes sat down and glanced at the two men before he spoke.

'I'm Wes Carter,' he said. 'I couldn't help but overhear your conversation with the barman. I think the man you're looking for is Vance Brady!'

The two men stiffened. 'What do you know of Brady?' asked the dark man cautiously.

Wes smiled. 'Wal, before I say any more I reckon I should know who I am dealing with,' he said, trying to play it big in front of this man.

'I'm sorry,' apologised the man with the moustache laying a restraining hand on his companion who seemed to take offence at Carter's observation. 'I'm Mel Walker and this is Butch Nolan. Now we know each other, do you have any information on Brady?'

'I ran foul of him today,' said Wes noting the excitement that came into Walker's eyes at the news which meant that Brady was not far away.

'Here in Tulia?' asked Mel eagerly.

'No,' replied Wes, but made no further attempt to offer information.

'I'll pay you well for news of his where-abouts,' said Mel.

Wes smiled. 'You told the barman you were his friends,' he said, 'but I figure that Brady has no friends following him. I'll be straight with you, Walker, I'm a bounty hunter and I'm interested in Brady because there is a price on his head. Now I reckon you aren't in the same line of business as me so I...'

'We certainly aren't,' cut in Walker. His sharp mind had suddenly realised that if this bounty hunter moved in before him then his chance of finding the money from Chey-enne Wells would be gone. 'You can have him for the price on his head and I'll pay you well to tell me where he is and for you not to act before me.'

'I'll take you up on that,' said Wes, 'but if I give you this information how do I know that you won't double-cross me. As we both want him for different reasons I was figuring we could help each other.'

Mel smiled. 'In other words you can't take Brady on your own.'

101

Carter's face darkened at the insinuation. 'I'll take Brady any time I want,' he hissed.

'Then why not today when you met him?' grinned Walker. 'Why enlist our help?'

Wes realised that Mel had seen through him. 'All right,' he said, 'I need help to capture him, you want him for some reason an' I know where he is so let's come clean with each other.'

Mel pursed his lips thoughtfully for a moment. 'All right,' he said. 'I'm interested in the money he took from the Cheyenne Wells bank. Oh not for myself,' he hastened to add, 'but for the wife of Brady's accomplice. I figure she's entitled to a good share of that money. Now until I find out where it is I can't let any bounty hunter take him. When I'm through you can have him because it will suit me to have him out of the way without any killing.'

Wes did not answer immediately and as Mel watched him carefully he guessed Wes' thoughts.

'Don't git ideas about trying to knuckle in on my set-up,' warned Mel, his voice leaving no misunderstandings about what he meant. 'You could easily be eliminated.'

'All right,' agreed Carter. 'But I'm not prepared to part with the information yet.'

He realised that whilst he kept that to himself he still had a hold over these men. 'But don't worry, I've got someone keeping an eye on Brady. The day after tomorrow I will probably know more about Brady's activities and plans, when we can act accordingly.'

Chapter Seven

It was early evening when Vance Brady strolled into the café a short distance from the hotel, and chose to sit on a high stool against a long counter which ran almost the full length of one wall. A young woman came for his order and Vance judged her to be about twenty-six. She was pretty, her dark hair which curled in the nape of her neck framed a round face. Her blue eyes smiled a welcome as she came forward.

'What can I get you?' she asked.

'I think I'll hev...' started Vance. 'No, I'll let you choose my meal and if it is as charming as you appear to be it will be my gain.'

The young woman smiled. 'It's the first

time I've been compared to food,' she said.

'I mean it as a compliment,' Vance hastened to add.

'I'm sure you do,' she said and turned away. Ten minutes later she returned with a meal which opened Vance's eyes.

'I can see I'm goin' to enjoy this,' he said, 'and with you for company the enjoyment will be doubled. I've had a long ride these last few days and this is a feast after hard tack and beans.'

'You must be Vance Brady,' she said.

Vance nodded. 'News travels fast in Plainview,' he replied.

'It is not a big place,' pointed out the café owner, 'and after the disturbance this afternoon, well, what would you expect.'

'Then you know of my reputation,' Vance said, his face serious.

'I do,' she replied, 'but I judge people as I find them and I find you entirely different from what I expected, in fact you have raised my curiosity as to why a man who obviously has a charming manner, a man who does not look like a bank robber, should have taken that path. I would...' Suddenly she stopped, a disturbed look on her face. 'I am sorry, Mr Brady, I should not be so presumptuous. I say I take people as I find them and then start prying into your past.'

Vance smiled. 'Thet's all right,' he said, 'I suppose it was just natural curiosity but please don't call me Mister Brady, the name's Vance.'

'And I am Jane Elliot,' said the young woman, 'but everyone calls me Jane.'

'Good,' said Vance. 'I'll tell you that story some time but at the moment I'd like to enjoy this food.'

Jane smiled and walked away. When Vance had finished his meal he called Jane over. 'I've been deprived of pleasant female company for a long time; may I walk you home when you finish tonight?' he said.

Jane hesitated a moment. Things were moving rather fast; after all this man was a stranger in town and a convicted criminal, but somehow Jane didn't see him like that. She was curious to know more about him.

'I'd like that,' she answered. 'I'll be closing in an hour.'

When Vance left the café he returned to the hotel, freshened up and an hour later was entering the café again. Jane locked the door and poured out two cups of coffee. Vance watched her closely as she did so, admiring her beauty and pretty gingham dress.

'Jane,' he said as they sat down. 'Isn't this

a bit risky from the town's point of view – you here alone with an ex-bank robber on his first night in town and the door locked?'

Jane laughed loudly. 'Vance, it would in most places but the Plainview folk are a tolerant people who are not given to malicious gossip; there might be a few frowns but that's all and it will all soon be forgotten, besides, I think everyone knows me and know that unless I approved of a person I wouldn't be here alone with him.' She looked curiously at Vance. 'Tell me what you think of the people's attitude towards you.'

Vance looked at his cup thoughtfully for a moment. 'Well, I've never been down this way and I figured I wouldn't be recognised, but I had to pick the town where the sheriff was a brother of the lawman in Cheyenne Wells. When I was known I thought maybe the attitude would be one of quiet hostility but it's not.'

'Exactly,' said Jane. 'You are certainly preferred to that bounty hunter. This town puts a lot on the judgment of Sheriff Jed Owen and they saw his attitude to you and that was good enough for them.'

'Then maybe it is a good thing I was recognised,' replied Vance thoughtfully. 'If this town accepts me, when they know who I am, then I figure this is the place for me. I'm looking fer somewhere to settle and I liked the countryside around here, now after what you have said it settles the matter.'

'This means you are going straight,' said Jane.

Vance nodded. 'I made that resolution in prison. It was the first time I had lost my freedom and oh how I missed that. I swore I would never lose it again. That is why I can't go into three states and why I must watch for men like Wes Carter.' He paused. He found Jane easy to talk to and suddenly he blurted out. 'I'd like to tell you my story.'

Jane smiled her approval. 'I was only seventeen when my father died and left a considerable estate. I did not learn this for a year and by that time I was penniless; three bank managers, thinking I was little more than a schoolboy, cheated me of every dime. I paid them all a visit and took the money from their three banks; I figured it was rightfully mine. That started me off. Bank managers were a race I hated and had to harm and you will find that I've never robbed anything but banks.'

Jane did not speak for a moment then, looking straight at Vance said with all sincerity, 'I am glad you are thinking of settling down here.'

Vance escorted Jane to a neat little house on the edge of town and as he walked back to his hotel he felt sure he was going to find a new life in Plainview. He reminded himself that he had another mission in Texas and a duty to Della Jenkins, but he thought that if the sheriff was successful in finding a piece of land he would fix things up before moving on.

The next day when Brady visited the sheriff's office Jed was pleased to see him.

'I was just comin' to look fer you,' said Jed. 'You'll be pleased to know that I hev just the spread you're looking fer.'

'You've got on to this quick,' said Vance excitedly.

'Wal, I didn't say anythin' yesterday as I wanted to confirm it – Mrs Rogers at the Running J has hinted fer some time thet she might sell. I rode out to see her and she'll sell at the right price,' explained Jed.

'Good,' replied Vance. 'I'll meet her price and thanks a lot fer what you've done.'

'You must see it before you decide,' insisted the sheriff. 'Come on, we'll ride out now.'

The two men left the office and an hour later were pulling up outside the long low ranch-house set on a slight rise above the surrounding grassland. Mrs Rogers came out of the house to greet them.

'Mrs Rogers, this is Vance Brady, the man interested in buying your ranch,' said the sheriff.

'Pleased to meet you, m'am,' said Vance touching the brim of his sombrero.

Mrs Rogers, a woman of about forty-five, her face lined by recent trouble, smiled a greeting.

'I took the liberty of ridin' Mister Brady over some of the spread,' said the sheriff as the two men swung to the ground.

'Good,' replied Mrs Rogers. 'I hope you showed him the bad parts as well as the good.'

'He did,' said Vance, 'and I like what I've seen, just name your price.'

Mrs Rogers looked thoughtful. 'I don't really know,' she said. 'If only Gil were here.' A sadness came into her eyes. 'We had got things going nicely when he was thrown from his horse and killed,' she explained. 'I've tried to carry on but I've found it rather hard and my folks in St Louis have been pressing for me to return there.'

'Will you take ten thousand dollars?' asked Vance.

'Ten thousand dollars!' Mrs Rogers gasped. 'But it's not worth that, Mister Brady.'

'To me it is,' said Vance. 'I want a place near Plainview so that I can settle down.'

'You are more than generous,' said Mrs Rogers gratefully.

'Could you possibly come to town this afternoon?' Vance asked, and when Mrs Rogers agreed he suggested three o'clock at the bank.

'I don't want you to rush out of the place,' said Vance. 'Take your time and have the covered wagon to take your belongings.'

'I'll be out in a couple of days,' replied Mrs Rogers.

The two men were about to go when four cowboys rode up and pulled to a halt outside the bunk-house.

'Jim,' shouted Mrs Rogers, 'come over here and bring the others.'

'The four men walked to the ranch-house and Vance studied them carefully as they approached. They were typical hard-working cowboys, their jeans tucked into the top of riding boots, their tough woollen shirts open at the chest and a neckerchief tied loosely round their throats, their Stetsons were battered and dusty and two were well curled at the brim. But it was the man slightly in the lead of the other three that drew Vance's attention. He was slightly taller than the others and a little thinner. His face was long and narrow and had a look of meanness in it.

'Jim, I want you to meet Vance Brady. I've just sold the ranch to him,' said Mrs Rogers. 'Mister Brady, Jim Selby, my foreman.'

Vance extended his hand but Jim did not take it. There was a gleam of suspicion and annoyance in his eye as he glanced sharply at Mrs Rogers.

'But you can't!' he protested. 'I hoped...' He stopped, then stared hard at Vance. 'Vance Brady,' he whispered. 'You've sold out to a bank robber,' he snapped.

'The sheriff has explained all about him to me,' replied Mrs Rogers testily. 'He's paid for his crime and I find a man I like, a man who wants to settle down here so I sell him my ranch. It has nothing to do with you, Jim!'

Jim spun round as if slapped across the face. 'I was good enough to run this spread when Gil died and if you'd hev dealt me in as a life partner I'd hev made a mint of money for us both!' snarled Jim.

'I didn't love you,' retorted Mrs Rogers. 'In fact your approaches nauseated me. I only kept you on because I knew it would be hard to get rid of you and besides, Gil asked me to, just before he died, although I never knew why.'

'You're a fool to sell this...' snapped Jim.

'That's enough,' lashed back Mrs Rogers. 'If I stop here with you as foreman I'll be ruined, you'll force me to do things your way and my only course out will be to marry you.'

Jim stared wide-eyed at Mrs Rogers. 'You knew,' he hissed. 'You knew.'

'Yes,' rapped the ranch owner. 'I was not blind to the things you were starting to do, but I'll forget those now otherwise the sheriff might see fit to take you into custody; instead with Mister Brady's permission, I'll perform my last act as owner of the Running J.' She drew herself to her full height, her eyes ablaze. 'You're fired,' she snapped.

Jim crouched like some frenzied animal. 'You'll not live to hev Brady's money,' he snarled grasping for his Colt.

Vance, who had been watching the foreman carefully, lunged forward crashing into the man as the Colt jerked upwards. The impact sent Jim sprawling as he pressed the trigger and the bullet whined harmlessly into the house splintering the woodwork close to the door. Vance kept his balance and before Jim realised what was happening a sharp kick sent the gun spinning from his hand. He glared angrily at Brady as he twisted round.

Jed Owen moved forward, his Colt covering Jim. 'On your feet,' he snapped angrily. 'You can cool off in jail fer a few days.'

'Let him go, please,' intervened Mrs Rogers.

'He can cause trouble,' warned the sheriff.

'And he'll be worse if you take him to jail,' replied Mrs Rogers.

'All right,' agreed Jed reluctantly. He looked hard at the foreman who was slapping the dust from his clothes. 'Git out of here an' don't let me see you around here again.'

The foreman walked reluctantly to his horse and climbed slowly into the saddle and rode away.

'Thank you again, Mister Brady,' said Mrs Rogers. 'He was a good foreman until he got the wrong ideas.'

'How about you others?' said Vance looking at the three cowboys. 'Hev any objections to working with an ex-bank robber.'

'If you're all right by the sheriff an' Mrs Rogers then you're all right by us,' spoke up one of the men.

Mrs Rogers smiled. 'This is Pete,' she said to Vance. 'That's Sam and Red.'

Vance nodded. 'Good,' he said, 'I'm pleased you'll stay, but I guess we'll need another foreman.'

'Sheriff,' called out Red. 'How about Clem Winters. I hear he's finished trail bossin'.'

'Thet's a good idea,' said the sheriff, 'we'll call on him when we git back to town.'

The two men mounted their horses but Vance hesitated before he rode. 'Come into town tonight,' he called to the three men. 'I'll be in the saloon about seven.'

'What's Clem Winters like?' asked Vance as they rode back to Plainview.

'He'll make you a good man,' answered Jed. 'He's been with cattle all his life. Bit of a restless hombre but his wife's been wanting him to settle down, maybe this job will suit him.'

When they reached Plainview the sheriff led the way to a small house standing on its own and their knock on the door was greeted by a pretty woman in her middle forties.

'We'd like to see Clem,' said Jed.

Mrs Winters led them into a room where Clem was reading a paper. He pushed himself from his chair as they came in.

'Clem,' said Jed. 'I'd like you to meet

Vance Brady.'

Vance extended his hand but detected a slight hesitation on the part of Clem Winters. Clem covered it up quickly and took the hand in a firm grip.

'Pleased to know you,' he said. 'This is my wife Meg.'

'Vance has a proposition to put to you,' said the sheriff.

Husband and wife glanced at each other wondering what this stranger had to say which was of interest to them.

'I've just purchased the Running J from Mrs Rogers an' I'd like Clem to be my foreman,' explained Vance.

They both looked surprised at the offer but Vance noticed a gleam of excitement in Meg's eyes. The tough, rugged trail boss, whose weather-beaten face looked as if it had been chiselled by the wind and sun, hesitated.

'Wal, I don't know,' he said, 'but I...'

'Clem, this is just the chance we want,' interrupted Meg quickly, not wanting her husband to start thinking of objections.

'We'll be together,' she went on pressing her case quickly. 'No more riding those long weary trails to the north; no more waiting; no more lonely nights. Clem, you've got to say yes.' There was a pleading, hopeful look in her eyes.

'I'll pay you sixty dollars a month and build you a house out at the ranch,' said Vance to make the offer more temping.

Clem looked at his wife. 'Meg, I guess I owe it to you after all the time you've spent alone. All right, Mister Brady, I'll take it.' He held out his hand and the two men sealed the bargain in a firm grip of friendship.

Meg was so overjoyed that there were tears of happiness in her eyes. 'Thank you, Mr Brady,' she said sincerely.

As the sheriff and Vance took their leave he invited Clem to join them in the saloon that evening.

Twenty minutes later, on Vance's request, the sheriff was introducing him to the bank manager. Vance deposited the twenty-five thousand dollars he was carrying into two accounts, fifteen thousand into his first account and ten thousand in a second. He intended working off the first and leaving the second until all the Cheyenne Wells money was gathered together in one account. Although not revealing his intentions he arranged with the bank manager to close the accounts of Vance Webb in La Junta and

Lamar and to transfer the money to his account in Plainview, splitting each amount in a similar way. Vance also arranged the purchase of the Running J and when he left the bank he felt in a much happier frame of mind; he had found a place to settle and the people accepted him, but most of all there was Jane Elliot whom Vance realized he liked very much even after only one meeting. He hurried to the café eager to tell Jane about the Running J and he was pleased that she was interested and delighted at the news.

As he returned to the hotel he felt more settled in his mind, but once again the cloud of Cheyenne Wells rose before him and he knew that he would have no peace of mind until the matter was settled and he had done what he thought best for Della Jenkins and Tom Corby's widow when he found her.

Chapter Eight

Mavis Cameron was full of smiles when she swung round on the stool in front of her dressing-table to face Wes Carter as he entered her room. Her flimsy dressing-gown tied slackly at the waist fell partially open as she crossed her legs and leaned back against the dressing-table.

'Something's pleased you,' said Carter as he stepped towards her, letting his eyes move from her slippered feet up her shapely legs across her slim body to her dark eyes which flashed amusingly at him. He bent over her and with one hand holding the back of her head kissed her passionately. As their lips parted there was the smoulder of desire in his eyes.

She pushed herself away from the dressing-table, swung on to her feet and spun round to face Carter. Her eyes flashed teasingly.

'You came here for information, Wes,' she said. 'I've got it and other things may cloud your judgment for the present.'

Carter grinned. 'All right, Mavis, you're generally right. What have you learned about Vance Brady.'

'Seems he's going to settle down here,' she replied. 'He's bought the Running J, kept on three hands and engaged Clem Winters as foreman.'

'This is a surprise,' mused Carter. 'Looks as if a bank robber's tryin' to go straight. Suits us, it will be easy for you to keep tags on him and we can take him when the time is right. I've teamed up with a couple of hombres in Tulia.'

'What!' Mavis's eyes flashed with annoyance. 'Two more to split with; it won't be worth the trouble for what we'll get out of it.'

'Hear me out,' answered Wes. 'It seems the cash that Brady took from the bank in Cheyenne Wells was never recovered; Brady had a conscience about the fact thet his side-kick got killed and he wants to see thet the widow is all right. She's in deep with one of these hombres – a certain Mel Walker – an' he's playin' fer the lot. They've been trailin' Brady but lost him north of Tulia. I told them I knew where Brady was an' Walker offered a thousand dollars fer the information.'

'You didn't tell him?' asked Mavis, alarm showing in her voice.

'Of course not,' replied Carter. 'An' I won't until I think fit. When Brady makes a move we follow an' when they hev what they want they hand over Brady to me an' I collect the bounty money.'

'Bounty money! You fool!' snapped Mavis angrily. 'You have the chance to knuckle in on bigger stakes an' you pass it up.'

'Hold it, Mavis,' rapped back Carter. 'I'm not so dumb as you think. It had crossed my mind to do what you suggest but I'd rather play it smaller an' safer. The bounty money plus thet thousand will be nice pickin's fer you an' me. If I'd tried to horn in on Walker's schemes he'd hev got rid of me without any hesitation when he had found where Brady was, as it is I serve as a means of him being able to git Brady out of the way conveniently, an' at the same time I hev their help to git Brady.'

The anger had died slowly in Mavis' eyes as she listened thoughtfully to Wes. 'Maybe you're right,' she mused. 'What's the next move?'

'You keep an eye on Brady,' replied Wes. 'Thet should be easy through his cowpokes' visits to the saloon. I'll be in Tulia an' I'll ride in here every two days; if anything happens sudden like git word to me at the saloon in Tulia.'

Mavis produced a bottle of whisky and they drank to the success of their plans.

About the same time as Wes Carter and Mavis Cameron were planning his downfall Vance Brady strolled into the café to be greeted by a warm smile from Jane Elliot.

'I really came to talk to you,' said Vance, 'but I would like a cup of your splendid coffee.'

'It will be yours,' said Jane and went through into the kitchen to return a moment later with the coffee. 'And what do you want to talk to me about?'

'I've been lucky enough to get the Running J,' said Vance. He hesitated a moment as if searching for words. 'I haven't known you long, Jane, an' I hope you don't think me too presumptuous but I'd be mighty glad if you would take a ride out there with me, have a look round the house an' tell me how you think I should furnish it. You see, I've not had a home for so long.' Jane smiled, but before she could answer him Vance went on. 'I will not be offended if you refuse. I've been a criminal and I understand if you don't want to be seen with me.'

'I am honoured by the invitation, Mister Brady,' replied Jane quietly, 'and I will be ready to ride to the Running J at four o'clock. The fact that you have been on the wrong side of the law does not matter, what does matter is what you are now and I see a man who is charming and likeable and who I suspect desperately wants to forget the past.'

Vance looked thoughtfully at his cup. 'How right you are, Jane,' he said. 'I want to put my past behind me but I'm afraid I cannot do that altogether, at least not for a while.'

'Why not?' asked Jane, a note of concern in her voice. 'Plainview won't rake it up; if it's thet Wes Carter you're bothered about he left town and hasn't been seen again; besides, if he does return I'm sure the sheriff will see he doesn't bother you.'

Vance smiled. 'It's not Carter that I'm concerned about, nor men like him, but I've some unfinished business to attend to. Now I've got the Running J I would like to get everything fixed up there before I move on for a short while.'

Jane sensed that Vance's business concerned his bank raids. 'Can't you forget whatever it is, Vance? Must you go?'

'Yes, I must,' replied Brady. 'I would not have an easy mind if I didn't attend to it. I'll tell you about it some day. I'm sure you'll understand, in the meantime let's think about the Running J.' Vance swung off the stool. 'See you at four o'clock, your house.'

Jane nodded and watched Brady stride from the café. She was finding herself attracted to this man and the fact that he had been a criminal did not seem to matter. He was good-looking, only a few years older than herself, and was most polite and charming, and being in need of friends seemed to have found pleasure in her company.

Jane found these feelings strengthened throughout the succeeding days. She saw a lot of Vance and after Mrs Rogers had left she did a lot towards making the ranch-house homely and attractive. Vance found himself attracted to Jane and on more than one occasion he found himself on the point of asking her to marry him, but he always held back. The money from Cheyenne Wells kept pushing itself into his mind. He had found peace and contentment in Plainview, the people accepted him and he knew that on this point he owed a lot to the sheriff and to Jane. He believed he would find happiness here but he realised that must wait until he had settled the business with Della Jenkins and, the as yet unfound, Mrs Corby. Vance knew that, even though he did not want to, he must ride out of Plainview one day and continue his search. He felt he would never have contentment of mind until the matter was closed.

He threw himself energetically into the work of establishing his ranch. He soon realised he had a good foreman in Clem Winters, a man who knew the business from A to Z, and that his three cowboys were good, solid, reliable men. In their turn they admired Vance Brady, they realised he was no ordinary bank robber, in fact they soon did not think of that side of him. He was a good boss who would work alongside them and would have his fun with them without losing the respect they owed him as their employer.

Work went ahead on the buildings; the bunk-house was enlarged and made more comfortable; the house for Clem Winters and his wife was erected and the stables refitted. When he was satisfied that this side of his ranch was as he wanted it Vance thought about the stock. Shortly before his death Gil Rogers had sold his entire herd and now Vance Brady entrusted the buying of five hundred head to Clem Winters.

All this had been carefully noted by Mavis Cameron, who gained her information quite easily from the gossip around town and also from the unsuspecting cowboys when they visited the saloon. Wes Carter visited Plainview regularly without being seen and carried Mavis' information back to Mel Walker in Tulia.

One night when Carter paid his call on Mavis he found her a little perturbed.

'I'm beginning to wonder if he's not going to bother about that money,' she said.

'No man in his right mind would do so – not the amount of cash he took from Cheyenne Wells,' replied Wes.

'The point I'm coming to, Wes,' went on Mavis, 'is that there's a golden opportunity coming for us to get Brady. His boys are in the saloon now and they're leaving tomorrow with Clem Winters to buy cattle. They'll be gone about a week and Brady will be on his own.'

Carter looked thoughtful as he paced the room. 'I see your point,' he said, 'but if I try to take Brady I'll run into trouble from Walker. I know he's had his sidekick follow me an' I reckon he could easily put two and two together if I try to duck out on him. I wouldn't dare leave you here – Walker would stop at nothing to get on Brady's trail. He's getting impatient as it is; as a matter of fact I was figurin' on telling him where Brady is when I get back to Tulia tomorrow.'

Mavis looked thoughtful. 'Maybe you're right,' she said, 'we'd better continue to play this safe.'

When Wes Carter walked into Walker's room in the hotel in Tulia the following day he found him impatiently awaiting his arrival.

'You are later back today, Carter,' snapped Walker. 'What kept you?'

'More checkin' on Vance Brady,' replied Carter.

'I hope you've got some more definite news for us,' replied Walker irritably. 'I'm gettin' tired of hangin' around here.'

'I sure hev,' said Wes. 'I'm afraid Brady shows no sign of movin'.' He went on to tell how the ex-bank robber had settled down outside Plainview and how through Mavis Cameron he had kept check on Brady's movements.

Mel Walker listened intently until Carter had finished. He studied for a few moments

126

before answering. 'You've hed a nice little set up, Wes,' he said. 'A neat way of keeping tabs on Brady without raisin' his suspicion. I wonder what he's playin' at – he just can't forget that cash; he must move some time. He told Della he would be back but had something else to see to. Maybe this was it; to find a place to settle down.'

'There's a glorious chance to take him,' urged Carter. 'His foreman an' cowboys are leavin' today to fetch some steers, they're likely to be away a week.'

Walker recognised Carter's implication. His eyes narrowed and he looked searchingly at the bounty hunter. 'We made a bargain, Carter,' he hissed. 'Don't git ideas about changin' it!' He paused to let his meaning sink in. 'I figure things this way; from what Brady said to Della I reckon he's got thet money stacked away somewhere, if he's used some of it to buy this spread he'll maybe move soon to git the rest. I figure it won't do any harm to give him a push.'

'How do you figure on doing thet?' asked Carter curiously.

'A few mishaps could force him to dig deeper into his pocket,' answered Walker.

Carter smiled. 'An' force him to head fer that money,' he said.

'You catch on fast,' grinned Walker.

They discussed plans and later that afternoon three men rode out of Tulia in a southerly direction. On Carter's advice they made camp in a boulder-strewn hollow five miles north of Plainview and three miles east of the Running J.

The following morning Carter led the two men to Brady's ranch and from a safe position they surveyed the buildings. The only two people they saw were Mrs Winters and Vance Brady.

'This is goin' to be easy,' said Walker, a measure of satisfaction in his voice. 'We'll destroy the buildings first. Butch, you stay here, keep an eye on Brady, if he rides out report to me, I'll be back in the hollow. Carter, you hev a quick trip into Plainview, see if your girl friend has any more news.'

Carter and Walker moved away, leaving Butch to keep his watch on Brady's movements. Mavis Cameron was surprised to see Wes Carter again so soon but had nothing further to report except to say that Jane Elliot was giving a small party that night and it was most likely that Vance Brady would be there. Carter returned swiftly to the hollow pleased with this news.

'There'll be a hunt up after this raid,'

pointed out Carter, 'so Mavis has suggested we head for Plainview an' hide out at her place. The sheriff's not likely to look in town fer the raiders.'

'She's smart, that girl of yours,' grinned Walker.

The two men broke camp obliterating all signs of their presence there. When they joined Butch he reported that Brady was still at the ranch. They settled down to wait and the light was beginning to fade from the sky when they saw a smartly-dressed Brady leave his house, mount his horse and ride to the Winters' home. He had a few words with Mrs Winters before turning his horse and putting it into a steady trot in the direction of Plainview.

The three men allowed Brady plenty of time to reach Plainview with the result that it was dark as they moved towards the buildings. The only light to be seen came from the Winters' house and the three men walked their horses so that they made little sound. About two hundred yards from the ranch-house they halted and Carter and Nolan handed their reins to Walker before slipping away into the darkness. Nolan ran to the bunk-house whilst Carter hurried to the ranch-house. Finding the door unlocked,

Wes crossed the hall to the living-room where he found an oil lamp, the contents of which he emptied around the room. He followed the same procedure in the bedroom, sprinkling the oil on the bed and splashing the curtains. Carter waited for a few moments then struck a match and threw it on to the bed. The oil ignited with a sudden flare and the bed clothes caught fire immediately. The flames followed the trail of oil and in a matter of seconds the bed was a mass of fire which leaped up the curtains. Carter raced to the living-room where he threw a match into the pool of oil in the centre of the carpet. Even as he ran into the hall the timber house was rapidly becoming a raging inferno.

As Wes ran from the building he saw Nolan pounding from the bunk-house through the open door of which he caught a glimpse of leaping flames. Both men raced for the horses, leaped into the saddles and together with Walker thundered away from the blazing outbuildings in a northerly direction.

Startled by the sound of galloping horses Mrs Winters hurried to the window and was horrified when she saw two buildings on fire. The flames already had a firm hold and from their dancing light Mrs Winters made out three riders. She ran to the door but as soon as she got outside she knew there was nothing she could do to save anything in the buildings. As the flames roared skywards she realised the stable was in danger from flying sparks. She ran quickly to the building where she hurried from stall to stall releasing ten of the eleven horses. The animals automatically made for the entrance but as soon as they saw the fire they turned frightened. The leaders tried to turn back but were forced forward by the others. Screaming with terror they broke into a gallop, turned swiftly away from the danger and pounded across the grassland. Satisfied that they were safe Mrs Winters hurried to the remaining horse and saddled it quickly. She climbed into the saddle and rode out of the stable. Scared by the sight of the fire the horse shied but Mrs Winters handled it skillfully and quickly brought it under control, sending it round the stable so that the building was between it and the fire. She soothed the frightened animal, talking to it softly as she rode away from the ranch. Once she was satisfied that the horse had settled down she kicked it into a gallop and headed for Plainvew with all possible speed.

Jane Elliot's party was a success and Vance Brady was getting to know some of the leading citizens of the small community more closely. Suddenly the sound of a galloping horse being pulled up sharply at the front of the house caused a lull in the conversation. A moment later a loud banging was heard on the door. There was something about the noises which forebode trouble. Jane glanced anxiously at the sheriff, a look of bewilderment and alarm on her face. She hurried from the room as the urgent hammering started again. The sheriff, who was near the door, stepped into the hall after Jane, and Vance, who had been at the opposite side of the room, threaded his way amongst the people at the door. At the first loud knock a feeling that he was concerned in its urgence had swept over him.

Jane opened the front door and cried aloud when she saw a dust-covered, dishevelled Mrs Winters standing there gasping for breath, her eyes wide with anxiety.

'Mister Brady,' she panted.

Jane reached forward and grasping Mrs Winters by the arm helped her forward into the hall.

At the mention of his name Vance stepped from the room and some measure of relief swept over Mrs Winters when she saw him. People were already crowding from the room, filling the doorway.

'The ranch, Mister Brady,' Mrs Winter went on, 'it's on fire!'

A murmur of surprise and alarm came from the group of people. Vance stared incredulously for a moment, this was not true; this couldn't happen to his new place. Jane was horrified and looked disbelievingly at Mrs Winters who had sunk on to a chair. The sheriff's jaw tightened grimly, fate had dealt a cruel blow to Brady just as he was getting established. Then he was aware that Mrs Winters was speaking and knew he was wrong to blame fate.

'I heard horses,' she explained. 'When I went to the window the ranch-house and the bunk-house were on fire, and three men were riding away.'

'What!' gasped Vance. 'This was done deliberately?' He looked puzzled.

'There was nothing I could do,' went on Mrs Winters. 'I was frightened the fire would spread to the stables so I let the horses out and rode here.'

Vance stepped forward and patted Mrs Winters on the shoulder. 'You have done well,' he said soothingly. 'Thank you very much.' He turned and was suddenly trans-formed into a man of action. 'Doc,' he called, 'see that Mrs Winters is all right, please.' He looked at Jane. 'Can she stay with you for the night?'

Jane nodded. 'Of course,' she said.

Vance turned to the sheriff. 'Will you ride with me?' he asked.

'It's my job,' answered the sheriff grimly.

The two men took their sombreros from Jane who had lifted them from the hooks on the wall.

'Take care,' she said as she opened the door.

The two men hurried down the path and were soon galloping towards the Running J. It was a silent ride as they pounded through the night, each man toying with his own thoughts; Jed wondering why Vance Brady's ranch should be attacked and Vance feeling almost certain he could guess the reason.

Flames still flickered at the odd, charred post which stood gauntly amongst the smouldering embers. The two men pulled their horses to a halt in front of what had been the ranch-house and sat there staring at the ruins, a feeling of utter helplessness on them.

'Thank goodness Clem's house an' the

stables are all right,' muttered Vance. 'I'll be able to round up the horses in daylight.'

'There's not much we can do here,' said Jed, 'but we'd better make sure the fire's properly out before we leave.'

The two men found some buckets in the stable and carried water from the pump to the smouldering ruins. They did not let up on their task until they were satisfied that there was no chance of a flare-up.

Tired with their efforts they leaned against a fence staring grimly at the remains of the buildings.

'You'd better come to my place for the night,' offered Jed.

'Thanks,' replied Vance. 'I want a party of men out tomorrow, they can start work on a new bunk-house, I want it ready by the time Clem an' the boys git back with the cattle; they've got to hev a place to come to.'

'This is costin' you something,' observed Jed.

Vance laughed. 'I've plenty,' he replied. 'An' I'm determined to settle down here.'

'I reckon you hev,' agreed Jed. His voice hardened a little. 'But let me warn you, Vance, I'm a lawman; if I see any of thet cash knowin' it's from Cheyenne Wells I'm takin' it.'

'I guess you would,' replied Vance. 'But you won't see it. I intend to split the lot two ways.'

'Two ways?' The sheriff was curious.

'Yes,' said Vance, 'between the widows of the two men who were with me on thet raid.' Vance pushed himself from the fence. 'C'm on,' he added as if putting an end to that line of conversation. 'I guess we'd better head back to town.'

Jed Owen respected Vance's desire not to pursue the subject further. He felt that the ex-bank robber would trust him with the full story when the time came. They walked to their horses and swung into the saddles.

'I'll try and pick a trail up tomorrow morning,' said Jed, 'but I've not much hope of finding those coyotes. Any idea who it might be?'

'None,' answered Vance and kicked his horse forward, but as he rode back to Plainview he thought of the words of warning offered by the governor of the prison.

Chapter Nine

As Mel Walker led the way from the ranch he was well satisfied with their night's work and when they topped a rise about two miles away he pulled to a halt and turned in the saddle. There was a grin of satisfaction across his face as he watched the glow in the sky from the burning buildings.

'Wal, Mister Brady, maybe thet will make you move,' he muttered grimly to himself.

The three men rode steadily northwards for a considerable distance before turning west and gradually swinging back to Plainview. It was late and the town was quiet when they entered the saloon. Tying their horses to a rail they moved quietly inside and when Wes Carter tapped lightly on the door of Mavis' room the saloon girl quickly admitted them.

'I didn't expect to see you back tonight,' she said, surprise showing in her voice.

Wes grinned. 'Mavis, I'd like you to meet Mel Walker and Butch Nolan.'

Both men nodded. 'I'm pleased to meet you, Mavis,' said Mel smoothly. 'From what

Wes tells me you're pretty smart at gettin' information.'

'We jest fired the Running J,' put in Wes, a note of satisfaction in his voice.

'What!' gasped Mavis. 'So that's why there was such a commotion in town earlier tonight, but what are you doing back here? This is the last place you should be.'

Mel smiled. 'They won't think we'll be hidin' out under their noses,' he said. 'Can you put us up?'

'Sure,' replied Mavis. 'You can have two rooms along the corridor.'

'Good girl,' said Mel. 'Tomorrow we'd like you to git a line on Brady; after tonight's fire we hope he'll have to move out to get more cash. Wes, what about the horses?'

'Leave it to me,' put in Mavis quickly.

After showing the three men to the rooms they were to occupy she hurried to the saloon which was on the point of closing and was relieved to see old Ben Porter still there. Mavis crossed the floor and sat down beside him. Ben glanced up, a look of pleasant surprise coming to his face.

'Ben,' whispered Mavis, 'I want you to help me.'

'Sure,' grinned Ban. 'Anythin' fer you, Mavis.'

'There are three horses at the back of the saloon,' she told him in a low voice. 'I want you to take them one at a time, to the livery stable and look after them. I don't know how long you'll have to keep them but they may be wanted in a hurry.'

'Leave it to me,' replied the stableman. 'I'll see to it.'

'Good,' said Mavis, 'but there is one thing. You must keep quiet about it and not tell anyone.'

'Depend on me,' came the reply.

'I do,' Mavis flashed him a smile. 'There'll be a good reward for you,' she said 'if you do this without anyone knowing.'

Mavis returned to her room a few minutes later and Ben Porter left the saloon to carry out his task.

The following morning Vance recruited a party of men and supplies and started building a new bunk-house in readiness for the return of Clem Winters and the men with the herd.

It was shortly after noon when Sheriff Jed Owen rode up to the Running J.

'I'm afraid it was useless,' said Jed as Vance greeted him. 'I picked up their trail from here all right but about mid-morning I lost it. I scouted around but it was hopeless. All

I can say is that they were headin' north. Haven't you any idea who it could be?'

'None at all,' replied Vance. 'There's Wes Carter– bounty hunter; there's Jim Selby – sacked foreman foiled in his schemes on this place; or there are a hundred folk who'd like to get their hands on the money from the Cheyenne Wells bank.'

'But why fire this place?' asked the sheriff thoughtfully.

'Wal, I've been doin' some thinkin' whilst we've been workin' this morning,' replied Vance. 'Rule out Wes Carter – a bounty hunter wouldn't hev to go to this length. Jim Selby? Wal, I reckon he wouldn't hev the spunk to come back after what I saw of him.' The sheriff nodded his agreement. 'That leaves someone interested in the money from Cheyenne Wells; wal, I figure it this way. Supposin' someone's been keepin' an eye on me hopin' I might lead them to the money, they see me settlin' down here an', figurin' I heven't brought any money with me, try to force me to go for it by destroying this place – it takes cash to re-erect these buildings, you know. So you see it could be anybody.'

'Then if you stay they may hit at you again,' pointed out the sheriff.

'Sure,' replied Vance, 'but I'm goin' hev this place guarded.'

The sheriff pursed his lips thoughtfully. 'A good idea,' he said, and then added after a pause: 'If somebody knows you're settlin' here then thet somebody must be from Plainview.'

'Thet seems likely,' agreed Vance, 'but don't fergit I could hev been followed here.'

'Sure,' replied Jed, 'but apart from yourself I heven't seen any strangers around.'

Both men would have been more than curious had they known that at that moment Mavis Cameron had just returned to the saloon to report to three men who were waiting for her in her room.

'You haven't forced Brady to move,' she told them.

'What's been goin' on?' asked Wes. 'We heard a lot of ridin' in the street this morning.'

'Brady's taken a party of men to the Running J to start rebuilding,' she explained.

Mel Walker's face darkened. 'Then, he'll have to be hit again.'

'If he can buy these things he must hev the money with him,' pointed out Wes.

'Hardly likely,' replied Mel. 'He hadn't thet amount of money with him in Wagon

Mound. I made sure about thet, and we've been following him since then. Besides, since he was in Wagon Mound he's been travelling south; now Vance Brady was taken somewhere in the Raton pass area and it was always thought that he'd hidden the money just before he was captured.'

'I can tell you that Brady has paid for these on a banker's note,' put in Mavis.

Mel smiled. 'Good girl,' he praised. 'You're sure smart; you've got what it takes. Then Brady must be using other money which he's had transferred or goin' to transfer to the bank. He wouldn't dare to try to deposit a sum of money as large as that which he took from Cheyenne Wells bank. I figure he hasn't picked it up yet so we'll hev to work on him again.' He turned to Mavis. 'We'll want one horse from the stable. Butch, I want you to keep watch on the Running J, but make certain you aren't seen. If anything unusual happens report here, otherwise let us know when they leave for the night; what Brady puts up must come down.'

Butch nodded and ten minutes later was heading away from Plainview in the direction of the Running J. He circled until he was on the north side of the ranch and took up an advantageous position on a low rise from which he was able to keep the buildings under close surveillance.

The sun was low on the horizon when Butch saw Vance Brady call a halt to the work on the bunk-house and head back to town with the men. Nolan hurried to his horse and rode quickly to Plainview which he approached with care. He dismounted at the back of the saloon and a few moments later was making his report to Mel Walker and Wes Carter.

'Brady didn't pull all the men out,' Butch concluded. 'He left some guards.'

Mel Walker cursed as he paced up and down the room. 'I should have guessed thet,' he muttered. Suddenly he stopped, his eyes had a new light in them. 'Wal, I reckon we can hit Brady even harder than bothering with his buildings,' he said excitedly. 'We'll hit the herd thet Clem Winters is bringing in!'

Before daylight the following day the three men left Plainview and rode steadily in the direction of the approaching herd. Two days later the sight of a dust cloud was their first contact with the herd, and immediately Mel Walker began making plans. He was highly delighted when Clem Winters settled the herd for the night in a position which was advantageous to his schemes.

When they had made camp in a small hollow some distance from the herd, Mel Walker explained his plans to Wes Carter and Butch Nolan.

'We'll hit them hard and fast just before daylight,' he said. 'The important thing is surprise and to cause an immediate stampede before those cowpokes realise what is happening. It is essential we keep the steers running hard in a north-westerly direction. It is not a big herd and if we keep them at a fast run we can probably drive them over thet escarpment to the north-west.'

'I figure we can make it easier fer ourselves if we move in on their camp a bit earlier,' suggested Wes. 'There are six of them, so Winters must hev hired a couple of drovers. Two will be night riders an' I reckon we can deal with the other four whilst they are still asleep.'

'Good idea, Wes,' agreed Mel, 'the two with the herd will be an easy matter after that, but no killing.'

The two men nodded and they settled down for the night.

Mel Walker woke his two companions early and it was still dark when they neared the Running J camp. After securing their horses the three men covered their faces with their neckerchiefs and crept silently towards the sleeping forms.

Each took a man and, using their Colts as clubs, dealt effectively with them. Wes Carter moved on to the fourth man and when Wes turned to Walker they knew that their attack on the herd would go undisturbed.

'Couldn't be better,' smiled Walker. 'Now for the herd, Wes, Butch, you take a rider each.'

The three men ran back to their horses and once in the saddle headed for the herd at a swift pace. The two night riders, hearing the sound of approaching horses, came together.

'Clem's got them movin' early,' drawled one.

'Wal, I don't mind,' replied the other, 'I'm sure ready for my breakfast.'

Three riders loomed out of the darkness and before the Running J men realised they were strangers Wes Carter and Butch Nolan were upon them. Wes drew his Colt and rode close to his man who threw up his arm in a last second attempt to ward off the blow. Wes' Colt slashed downwards and the cowboy took most of the impact on his arm but the force was sufficient to send him reeling from the saddle. Pain tore at his arm and he crashed heavily to the ground. Wes hauled hard on the reins bringing his horse spinning round. He jumped from the saddle and leaped at the dazed man. One swift blow was sufficient to knock him out and immediately Wes leaped for his horse.

Butch Nolan had been more successful on the initial attack. He was on top of his victim before the cowboy realised his intention and Butch's aim was true. His Colt crashed across the side of the man's head dropping him from the saddle to lie still on the ground. Butch kept his mount going to pull alongside Mel Walker who was riding hard straight at the herd.

Already the steers were restless, frightened by the sudden pounding of hoofs and when Walker and Nolan, closely followed by Carter, neared them they started to move. Yelling at the tops of their voices and firing their Colts into the air, the three men urged the nearest steers into a run. Steer pushed against steer until the motion spread through the herd and the cattle broke into a dead run away from the frightening noise. Carter and Nolan moved on either side of the herd trying to keep the steers as compact as possible but not worrying if any broke away from the main bunch. The cattle stampeded wildly onwards urged by the three men. After a four-mile run they were nearing the edge of the escarpment and Carter and Nolan dropped back to help Walker push them forward. Scared, bellowing steers tried to turn when they reached the drop but the pressure of the herd behind them sent many of the leaders plunging over the edge. Only those on the sides of the herd were able to turn whilst those in the centre in their attempt to move away pushed against each other, their horns ripping and gashing the hides of their neighbours. Steer after steer plunged madly, bellowing with fright whilst all the time the three men exerted their pressure from behind. Suddenly the herd seemed to split into two waves as cattle on either side gave way to the thrust from the centre and those which had not plunged to their deaths split across the grassland in an earth-pounding gallop. The three men drew their panting horses to a stop and, released from the tension of the ride, they slumped in the saddles recovering their breath.

Mel pulled the neckerchief from his face and wiped the dust away. 'I reckon there's a few cattle thet won't see the Running J and many of those still on their feet are badly hurt. If Brady's to replace them he'll need more cash; maybe this will make him move.' He pulled his horse round. 'C'm on, let's ride fer Plainview.'

The light was beginning to break the eastern horizon as the three men put their horses into a steady pace well satisfied with their work.

Clem Winters stirred; his head pounded as if a hundred hammers were beating inside it. His eyes flickered open, everything was in a daze but he was aware of a brightness. Slowly his mind cleared and he realised it was daylight. What had happened? He was still wrapped in his blankets. With an effort he raised his arm and felt his head and was startled by a lump and the sticky feel of blood. Clem pushed himself into a sitting position and, as the effort made his head spin, he sat for a few moments holding his head until it cleared again. He glanced round and saw one of his cowboys stirring but the other two were still unconscious. The sudden realisation of what must have happened seemed to drive strength into him. He reached for his canteen and, uncorking it, poured water over his head, finding refreshment in its coolness. He pushed himself to his feet, then froze when he realised the herd was no longer there! This galvanised him into action; he examined his men and was relieved to find that apart from being knocked unconscious they had suffered no harm. He revived them quickly and had them in the saddle as soon as he could. As they headed across the grassland Clem was worried about the two night-riders, but his mind was eased when he saw them riding towards him.

'What happened?' he asked as they pulled to a halt.

'Some hombres hit us,' replied Red. 'We thought it was you coming and they were on us before we saw that it wasn't.'

'They sure timed it right,' muttered Clem. 'Still dark enough to hide them. Did you get a glimpse of them at all?' he added hopefully.

Red shook his head. 'No, all we can say is there were three of them,' he answered.

'Three smart ones,' observed Clem. 'They took us whilst we were still asleep so none of us got a look at them. C'm on, we'll see if we can trail them.'

The six men had no difficulty in following the path of the herd and as they neared the edge of the escarpment Clem was filled with horror, but he did not voice his thoughts until they were on the edge of the drop.

'Looks as if they had no intention of rustlin' the herd,' he said grimly, 'otherwise they wouldn't hev headed in this direction. I reckon there's nearly half the beeves down there,' he added, as he peered over the edge, 'the rest will be scattered far and wide.' He paused for a moment, his face grim. 'What a way to start a first job for Vance Brady,' he muttered dejectedly.

'Wal, I reckon he'll understand,' comforted Red.

'I guess so,' said Clem, 'but I wonder who would want to destroy his cattle, and why?'

'Any chance of followin' them?' asked one of the hired hands.

'I reckon not,' answered the foreman. 'Too many cattle marks about. I think I'd better head fer Plainview and see Brady. I'll be back, in the meantime round up as many of the cattle as you can find.' He went on to issue instructions then headed for Plainview with his grim news. Clem kept his horse to a fast pace for most of the day. It was a long ride and he conserved the animal's energy as best he could whilst keeping the urgency of the situation in his mind. It was dark by the time he reached the Running J and so intent was he on getting to the house that he did not notice the ruins until he was almost on top of them. The shock was so great that he automatically hauled hard on the reins bringing the tired animal to a sliding halt. He stared in amazement at the ruins hardly able to believe his eyes. Sudden panic seized him and he turned in the direction of his own house but relief came to him just as suddenly when he saw that the building was undamaged. His eyes swept across the stables and settled on the new bunk-house which was almost completed alongside the ruins of the old.

'Hold it right there or I'll blast you right out of the saddle!' a voice rasped through the darkness.

Clem halted his horse and froze in the leather. His eyes tried hard to locate the person behind the voice but he could not and he reckoned whoever it was was somewhere near the new bunk-house.

'All right, Sam,' said the voice again. 'I've got him clean in my sights; see who it is.'

Clem tensed himself as a shadowy figure appeared from the bunk-house and came towards him. He approached cautiously and stopped a few yards from the horseman.

'Frank, it's Clem Winters,' Sam called over his shoulder, a measure of relief in his voice.

Sam and Frank Easby! The words flashed in Clem's brain. Sam was already stepping towards him.

'Clem Winters,' he called, 'what are you doin' here?'

'I could ask you the same,' replied Clem swinging from the saddle.

'Place was burned down the other night by three hombres,' explained Sam as they walked towards the bunk-house. 'Brady wanted the bunk-house up by the time you got back.'

'Who were they?' asked Clem.

'Don't know,' answered Sam. 'Your wife's all right and is staying in town with Jane Elliot.'

Frank and Clem exchanged greetings as Frank came from the bunk-house to meet them. 'You look all in, Clem,' said Frank. 'What's happened to you?'

Clem explained quickly. 'Where's Brady?' he asked when he had finished his story.

'He's stayin' at the sheriff's,' replied Sam. 'I'll git you another horse from the stable whilst you hev some coffee.'

Clem was back in the saddle as soon as possible and heading at a fast gallop for Plainview. He did not spare the horse on the shorter run and it was not long before he was pounding along the main street. He saw that the sheriff's office was in darkness and headed straight for his house.

It was a surprised Jed Owen who let Clem into the house and took him into a room where Vance Brady jumped from his chair when he saw his dust-stained, travel-weary foreman.

'Clem! What's happened?' he cried.

'The herd was hit and stampeded this morning,' Clem replied.

'What!' Vance stared incredulously at Clem.

Winters went on to explain what had happened. 'I'm afraid the herd's been badly mauled,' he concluded. 'Half of them lost and I expect a lot of the others badly hurt. I'm sorry, boss.'

'It wasn't your fault,' said Vance, 'so don't worry.'

'My first job fer you an' I slip up,' muttered Clem dejectedly, the strain of the raid and the ride made themselves felt.

'You hev nothin' to reproach yourself for,' insisted Vance. 'You've seen what has happened at the ranch,' he went on. 'Your wife is with Jane Elliot. I'll take you round there, she'll look after you, then we'll talk things over in the morning.'

The two men moved towards the door when the sheriff stopped them.

'How many men attacked the herd?' he asked.

'Three,' answered Clem.

The sheriff and Vance glanced sharply at each other.

'Recognise any of them?' questioned Jed.

Clem shook his head. 'I'm afraid not,' he said. 'As I told you, they took us whilst we were asleep and the two men guarding the herd were jumped so fast thet they hadn't time to recognise anyone, besides, they had neckerchiefs over their faces and it still wasn't light.'

The sheriff looked seriously at Vance.

'Must be the same three that burned the ranch,' he said. 'Someone's determined to hit you hard.'

Vance had much to think about on his way back from Jane's, but of one thing he was certain, he was determined to triumph over these troubles.

Chapter Ten

The next day Vance accompanied Clem
Winters when he rode back to what remained of the herd. Vance was more than
pleased to find that the cowboys had
rounded up approximately half of the ori-
ginal number of steers. The drive back to
the Running J passed without mishap and
when they reached the ranch Vance was
delighted to find that the bunk-house had
been completed. After they had all enjoyed
a meal which Mrs Winters had prepared for
them Vance rode into town to see the
sheriff.

'I'm sorry, but I haven't found anything
which could give us a lead on your attackers,' said Jed in reply to Vance's enquiry.
'It's a mystery to me. They must hev a
perfect hide-out but the thing thet really
puzzles me is that they hev been able to
keep a close check on your activities.'

'Then thet points to someone in Plainview,' said Vance.

The two men discussed the matter fully

but could get no nearer to solving the problem.

'I wish you'd strap back your gun,' said the sheriff as Vance was leaving.

Brady shook his head. 'It's not necessary,' he replied. 'They won't attack me, remember we figure they want me to lead them to the money.'

Throughout the following four days the sheriff kept up his search for a lead but was unsuccessful. The work on the new ranchhouse went ahead rapidly and when it was finally completed Vance called Clem Winters in.

'I want you to take the boys tomorrow and go to pick up another herd,' he instructed.

'Is it wise?' asked Clem. 'I know things hev been quiet since the herd was attacked but it could happen again.'

'It's a chance we'll hev to take,' replied Vance. 'Hire more men fer the trip if you like and keep a sharp lookout. I doubt if they'll try it a second time. Besides, I think I know what they are after so it might be a good idea if I ride out of here. It could easily lead them away.'

'There's no need to do thet,' said Clem. 'We'll handle them if they try to take the herd again.'

Vance smiled at the determination in the deep voice and he knew he could rely on Clem Winters to get this herd through without any bother.

'Thanks, Clem,' said Vance. 'I don't really want to move yet as there are one or two things I want to see to. Tell the boys now; they might like to have the night in town before they hit the trail tomorrow.'

'I'm sure they will,' said Clem with a smile as he left the house.

Mel Walker was getting impatient with the fact that Vance Brady seemed to show no inclination to move.

'It must be costing him a packet,' he pointed out to Wes Carter and Butch Nolan. 'He's got to move to get thet money.'

'Wal, I figure it's time we started on Brady himself,' said Wes. 'Nolan looks as if he could persuade a man to talk.'

Butch grinned. 'I sure could,' he drawled.

Mel Walker looked thoughtful. 'Anything is worth a try,' he said, 'but it will need careful planning.'

At that moment the door opened and Mavis Cameron hurried in. 'I've news for you,' she said with a smile. 'Brady's cowpokes are in the saloon for a night out before they hit the trail tomorrow for more cattle.'

'This could be just what we want,' said Wes excitedly. 'When they've gone he'll be at the ranch on his own.'

'Right,' agreed Mel, 'we'll try it. We'll keep watch on the Running J.'

The next day they watched Clem Winters lead the Running J cowboys away from the ranch and shortly afterwards Mrs Winters went to town to stay with friends until her husband's return.

'Couldn't be better,' grinned Mel. 'We'll wait until it's dark and then our approach will be unnoticed.'

A light shone from the ranch-house as the three men, their faces well covered with neckerchiefs, rode quietly to the front of the house. They tied their horses to the rail, stepped on to the veranda and knocked loudly at the door. A few moments later a surprised Vance Brady was pushed roughly back into the house.

'What's the idea?' he gasped looking round the three men who covered him with Colts.

'We just want some information,' snapped Walker. 'Now you can either give it to us quietly or...'

He left the sentence unfinished knowing full well that Brady would know what he meant. To add meaning to the spoken words Butch had slipped his Colt back into its holster and was slapping his right fist into the palm of his left hand.

Vance looked round desperately. Could he make a dash for it? His thoughts raced, but he decided it would be an attempt in vain. He must try to play for time to give him a chance to outwit these men.

'I have no information worth anything,' he said.

'I reckon you have; something that must be worth close on sixty thousand dollars,' replied Walker.

'So I was right,' said Vance quietly. 'You've been tryin' to smoke me out to lead you to the Cheyenne Wells money.'

'You're smart, Brady,' congratulated Walker. 'Now keep smart and tell us where it is.'

'You've really got desperate if you've come to this,' said Vance. 'Got tired of waitin' fer me to move?'

'Cut out the rambling,' snapped Walker. 'Where's thet money?'

'I doubt if I can find it myself,' replied Vance.

'Don't give me thet,' rapped Walker, a note of irritation in his voice. 'You don't stack that amount away without being certain where you put it. Somewhere near Raton Pass, wasn't it?'

Brady did not answer.

Walker's eyes narrowed. 'Then we'll have to beat it out of you,' he hissed and nodded to Nolan who stepped slowly towards Brady.

Vance tensed himself, his fists clenched tightly.

'Don't try anythin',' snarled Wes. 'I'd hate to put a bullet in your leg.'

'I'll do thet if necessary,' put in Mel coldly. 'Put your gun away and give Butch a hand.'

Wes grinned and slid his Colt back into its holster. 'It will be a pleasure,' he said recalling how he had been outsmarted by Brady.

Vance's face was grim as he faced the two men. Who were they? If only he could get a glimpse of their faces. His brain pounded as he looked for some clue, then his eyes rested on Carter's holster and the smooth butt of the Colt and he knew this man had tackled him before!

Suddenly Wes moved behind him, grabbed him and locked his arms tightly holding him at the mercy of Nolan. Butch swept the back of his huge hairy hand hard across Vance's face. His head jerked sideways and a searing pain shot through his head. Butch's fist came up smashing his face on the other side, opening a cut across his cheek from which the blood began to trickle.

'Talk?' hissed Wes in his ear. 'Or do you want more?'

Vance's answer was to kick out with his right foot, catching Nolan under his left knee. Butch grunted with pain; his eyes flashed furiously. He lunged forward angrily, driving his fist hard into Vance's stomach. Brady gasped as a second blow sent the breath from his body. He tried to double up but Wes Carter held him firmly. Pain stabbed through his body as Nolan pounded his fists into him. He began to go limp, then Wes released his hold allowing him to slump on the floor. Vance groaned, holding his stomach, gasping for breath. Butch drew back his foot but Walker stepped forward to stop him.

'Enough for the moment,' he said. 'Well, Brady, prepared to talk?'

Vance shook his head. 'You'll never get to know.' He panted each word with an effort.

Wes, who was standing over him, clenched his fist and hit him hard across the side of the head propelling Vance on to his back. He stared upwards unable to protect himself as Nolan stepped forward. The big powerful man grasped him by the front of the shirt and jerked him upwards, then smashed fist into mouth, sending him crashing backwards on to the floor.

'Talk!' he screamed.

'Hold it,' said Mel, alarm showing in his voice. He inclined his head, listening intently. 'There's someone comin'. Let's get out of here.'

The faint clop of horses' hoofs sounded in the distance. The three men tore out of the house, leaped on to their horses' backs and galloped away into the darkness.

Jed Owen and Jane Elliot were startled when the quietness of the Texas night was suddenly broken by the sound of hoofs pounding away from the Running J ranch-house. The night was dark and they were too far away to make anything out.

'What's that?' gasped Jane, alarm in her voice.

'I don't know,' replied Jed, 'but I don't like it. C'm on.'

He pushed his horse into a gallop, closely followed by Jane, and alarm seized him when he saw the door of the house was open. He jumped out of the saddle, leaped up the steps on to the veranda and ran into

162

the house. Jed pulled up sharply when he saw the battered form of Vance Brady sprawled on the floor. Jane gasped with horror, her eyes widening with alarm when she saw Vance. They dropped on their knees beside him and after a swift check of the unconscious man Jed was satisfied that as far as he could ascertain no serious damage had been done.

'I reckon he'll be all right,' he said, re-assuring Jane. 'We'll git him on to a bed.'

A few moments later Jed was stripping Vance's shirt from him and when Jane arrived with some hot water she bathed his wounds gently. Jane spent ten anxious minutes and was relieved when Vance began to stir and opened his eyes. He looked round vaguely and winced when he felt the aches in his body. His cheeks felt puffed and his swollen lips hurt when he touched them with his tongue. His gaze rested on Jane and he smiled weakly as his brain cleared and he recognized her. Jed hurried into the room with a bottle and supported Vance whilst Jane gave him a drop of brandy.

Vance struggled to sit up but Jed made him lie still until he gained more strength. When at last he was able to get up Jed helped him to his feet and gave him support as they walked into the other room.

'It's a good job Jane and I arranged this visit for tonight,' he said as Vance lowered himself gently into a chair.

'I'm mighty glad you arrived when you did,' said Vance. 'I reckon you scared them off.'

'We heard them ridin' away,' replied the sheriff, 'but I'm afraid we didn't get a sight of them. Any idea who it was?'

'Wal, I didn't git a look at them,' answered Brady. 'They hed their faces covered, but I'm pretty certain one of them was Wes Carter.'

'What!' gasped Jed. 'I thought we'd seen the last of thet no good bounty hunter.'

'I recognized his Colt and holster from thet first day in Plainview,' said Vance. 'I hev an eye for weapons.'

'You should have been wearing one,' put in Jane, 'then this probably wouldn't have happened.'

'I told him that before,' said Jed, 'but he wouldn't take my advice. Why should a bounty hunter beat you up?'

'It looks as if he's thrown in with someone else,' explained Vance. 'The hombre thet really sank his fists into me was a rough, tough coyote, sidekick of the third man who did all the talkin', I reckon, an' he was only interested in the Cheyenne Wells money. Seems I wasn't far off the mark when I reckoned they were trying to force me to leave for more money.'

Jane was puzzled and the men explained their theories about the attacks.

'We can't leave Vance here,' she said when they had finished. 'These men may return.'

'Quite right, Jane,' said Jed. 'Vance can come back to town and stay with me. Think you can manage the ride?'

Vance nodded and half an hour later the three friends rode slowly to town.

Vance Brady did not rest easily that night. His body ached, but more than that his thoughts about the recent events and the future troubled him. However, by the time morning came he had come to a decision and over an appetizing breakfast, he spoke frankly to the sheriff.

'I've been doin' a lot of thinkin',' he said, 'an' I figure that as long as I stay here there will be trouble, other people will be involved and it is not fair to them, so I reckon I will move on.'

Jed looked at Vance sharply. 'There's no need fer thet,' he said. 'We can handle any trouble thet comes along.'

'I know that,' replied Vance, 'but don't you see, someone might git killed because of me. I'll be all right because they want me alive, but I should hate to be the cause of anyone getting hurt. My cowboys have already had a taste; now supposin' they tried to get at me through Jane; how do you think I'd feel?'

'I see your point,' said Jed thoughtfully. 'But what about the Running J; you're just gittin' nicely settled there, and what about Jane? I know you two have been seeing a lot of each other and you don't do that unless there's something serious in it.'

Vance smiled. 'Has it been as obvious as that?'

'Wal, I can't answer fer you,' said Jed, 'but I do know Jane thinks an awful lot about you.'

'Look, Jed,' replied Vance seriously. 'I love Jane enough to ask her to marry me but I want to get this other thing settled first.' Vance paused, wondering how much he should tell Jed seeing that he was a lawman. Before he could go on Jed spoke.

'I think there is somethin' you should know, Vance,' Jed's voice was hesitant.

'Let me finish first,' put in Vance, having made up his mind to take Jed into his confidence. 'When I got away with the money

166

from Cheyenne Wells I made deposits in three separate banks; never mind how and why I was able to do that; but I still had thirty thousand with me when the sheriff of Rocky Ford got on my trail. I managed to hide it just before I was caught, so you see if these three hombres follow me to that money there is not the amount they are expecting. Now I propose to lead them to it but I'll see they don't git it, because I'm goin' to lump all the Cheyenne Wells money together an' split it between the widows of the two men who were killed on the raid.'

'What about the money you've spent since comin' here?' asked Jed.

'Not one dollar of that was from Cheyenne Wells,' explained Vance. 'It was all mine. I'm not tellin' you where I've got the Cheyenne Wells money because I know you'd do your duty as a lawman and do what you could to get your hands on it and return it.'

Jed nodded grimly. 'I would,' he said firmly. 'Why not return it, Vance, if you've got sufficient of your own. Thet would stop these hombres when it became known.'

'I'd thought of thet,' replied Vance, 'but I'm haunted by the death of two men. I found the widow of Ace Jenkins working in a saloon in Wagon Mound in New Mexico. She'd had a pretty rough time and in some way I feel I'm to blame. With what I can give her she can get out of that place and be well off; I feel that might be some sort of compensation.'

'I can guess how you feel,' said Jed, his face serious. 'What about the other one, know where she is?'

Vance shook his head. 'All I know is she's somewhere in Texas, at least I expect so. Ace Jenkins picked up a young drover who had lost all his pay at the end of the drive and had nothin' to return with to his wife in Texas. He'd got married just before he'd trailed north, Ace wanted to count him in on the robbery. I agreed against my better judgment – the result you know.'

'His name never came out at your trial,' said Jed.

'I didn't want to disclose it. I thought it might break his wife's heart,' explained Vance. 'After all, he was no thief really.'

'Thet was mighty thoughtful of you,' said Jed.

'I'll hev to think of some story to tell her when I find her,' mused Vance. 'I guess she'll hev wondered what happened to her husband; his name was Tom Corby.'

Jed gasped, taken by surprise at this name. He looked hard at Vance, his eyes wide with amazement. 'Tom Corby!' he whispered.

'Yes,' replied Vance, surprised at the effect the name had on the sheriff. 'Did you know him?'

Jed nodded. 'Sure.' He paused; his thoughts raced wondering just how to tell Vance what he knew. 'Before you told me this story I said there was something you should know – wal, now' – Jed hesitated. 'You'll see what I mean when–, wal, Tom Corby's widow lives in Plainview.'

'What!' Vance's eyes lit up with excitement. 'How lucky can one be? Where does she live?'

'Now hold hard,' said Jed seriously. 'I was going to tell you that Jane Elliot is a married woman but that she hadn't heard of her husband for five years and that there would be things to clear up before you and she–'

Vance stared wide-eyed at the sheriff as the meaning behind Jed's words thrust itself forward. 'You don't mean–?' he interrupted.

Jed nodded. 'Jane is Mrs Tom Corby,' he said quietly.

'But … but … I don't understand,' spluttered Vance, still hardly able to believe Jed's words.

'This is Jane's home town,' explained Jed, 'and it was here that she met and married Tom Corby. They went south to live and it was nearly a year later that she returned to Plainview when her husband didn't return from a cattle drive to Ogallala. She lived with her parents and, as everybody here knew her as Jane Elliot, they'd only known her as Corby on her wedding day, and kept calling her that, she went on using her maiden name. Her parents died about two years ago and it was then that Jane opened the café.'

Vance, his thoughts tumbling one on top of the other, could not speak. He stared at the sheriff incredulously. The sheriff respected his silence; he knew what a shock this must have been to Brady. A few minutes passed before Vance spoke.

'What am I to do?' he whispered half to himself. 'I hoped to come back and marry Jane, but now that's impossible, she'll hev nothin' but contempt for the man who caused her husband's death.'

'Need she know?' asked Jed.

'What do you mean?' Vance was puzzled.

'She could get her husband declared dead legally and then you and she could get married without…'

'I couldn't do that knowing what I do

170

about Tom's death,' said Vance.

'You can't pretend her husband is alive and say the money is from him,' pointed out Jed. 'She'd want to know where he was, want to go to him – that way would be cruel to a girl like Jane.'

'Then there is only one thing to do, tell her the truth, see that she is provided for and then get out of here and let her forget me,' said Vance.

Jed Owen started to protest but Brady stopped him. 'I've made up my mind, that is the only thing to do in fairness to both of us.'

The sheriff shrugged his shoulders. 'I guess this is somethin' only you can work out,' he said. 'But remember this, I hope you'll find some solution and stay at the Running J.'

In spite of the fact that he had been emphatic about his decision, before he left the sheriff, Vance was plagued with doubts as he approached Jane's café. He felt numb inside as he pushed open the door and walked to one of the high stools beside the counter. He wished he could wake up and find it was all a dream, but there was Jane smiling a greeting.

'Hello, Vance,' she said brightly. 'How are you feeling?'

'All right,' replied Vance.

There was no enthusiasm in his voice and Jane was puzzled by the glum look on his face. She brought him a cup of coffee and he sipped at it without speaking.

'What's the matter, Vance?' she said. 'Are these raids getting you down?'

Vance just shook his head. Suddenly he put down his cup, grabbed his sombrero, swung from the stool and started for the door. Jane stared after him in amazement. Suddenly Vance stopped, turned round and walked slowly back to her.

'Jane,' he muttered quietly, 'I'm sorry for being unsociable, please forgive me, but I've learned something this morning which is worryin' me. When I started to go out of here just now I thought I could walk away from it but I realised I couldn't.'

'What is it, Vance?' asked Jane, her voice sympathetic. 'If there is anythin' I can do you've only got to say.'

Vance smiled weakly, looking hard at the pretty girl. He wanted to spare her any pain and yet would it be fair not to tell her? 'Jane, I've a lot of things to tell you, can you shut the café?' he said.

'But there are customers here,' said Jane, 'and about noon it gets busier. Can't it wait?'

'Wal, I guess it can,' said Vance. 'What about this evening?'

'I'll close early,' replied Jane. 'Come to my house about six. I'll have a meal ready for you there, then you can tell me all about it.' She smiled warmly.

Vance agreed and walked from the café, leaving a puzzled Jane wondering what troubled him and also trying to reach a decision herself.

She had strong feelings about Vance and she thought that he liked her, but she felt she could not encourage him without telling him about her husband. Tonight might be a good time to tell him.

Chapter Eleven

Vance approached Jane's house with mixed feelings that same evening but when he found himself seated in front of a most appetising meal with Jane on the opposite side of the table he felt more at ease and he knew it was his duty to tell the truth.

'Well, Vance, I think we will have our meal before we talk; since seeing you this morning

I have decided that tonight I, too, must tell you something which I have been reluctant to face.'

Jane's voice was quiet and Vance was only too pleased to agree to her suggestion.

When the meal was over Jane led the way into the next room where a roaring fire lent a relaxing atmosphere to the evening. Vance sank into a chair and stretched his legs in front of him realising that this was the type of home he had hoped would be his at the Running J but which in a few minutes would be lost forever. When Jane had brought in the coffee and had seated herself in a chair in front of the fire Vance came straight to the point.

'I have a terrible confession to make to you, Jane,' he said seriously, 'but no matter what I say now, please believe me that since I came to Plainview I have tasted happiness being with you. I love you very much, Jane, please remember that, no matter what happens.'

'Please don't, Vance.' There was a tone of anguish in Jane's voice. 'Don't say nice things to me, you see, I am already married.' The words had come out almost before she realised it. She looked at Vance intently but there was no sign of surprise on his face.

'I know,' he said quietly.

'You knew?' gasped Jane.

'I only learned this morning,' replied Vance.

'From Sheriff Owen?' asked Jane.

'Yes,' answered Vance, 'but only because it related to things I told him, and those things I must now tell to you.' He paused a moment as if gathering his thoughts. There was a pitying look in his eyes when he looked at Jane. 'You see,' he went on, 'I know your husband is dead.'

Jane gave a little gasp. 'Tom, dead! Somehow I've had that feeling for a long time. I seem to have known all along that I would never see him again. It comes hard but somehow it is not as hard as I expected; I have been without him for so long. In fact I suppose I hardly knew him at all. Our marriage was a whirlwind affair and before long he had to head north on a cattle drive. But how did you know him, Vance?'

Vance licked his lips. Jane had taken the first part of his news well but now he realised she was to hear something which would shock her. He wished there was some other way.

'The night before Cheyenne Wells,' explained Vance, 'I kept a rendezvous with my partner Ace Jenkins. When Ace arrived he brought with him a young drover whom he introduced as Tom Corby. Ace had met Tom in Ogallala; it was after the drovers had received their pay for the drive; Tom, apparently thinking he could increase his pay so that he could come back to you with sufficient to really improve your home, got into a card game. Things went the wrong way and trouble was brewing when Ace pulled Tom out. He'd lost his cash and the prospect of having to return with nothing did not please him. Ace persuaded me to take him to Cheyenne Wells with us and split him in with whatever we got.'

Jane stared incredulously at Vance; she was speechless. Her lips quivered; tears began to fill her eyes.

'I'm sorry to say the raid went wrong and Tom got killed.' Vance paused. 'No, I must tell you exactly what happened. We got the money but the sheriff, Jed's brother, was in the street when we came out of the bank; Tom panicked and drew his Colt. He'd hev killed the sheriff if I hadn't knocked his arm, thet of course enabled the sheriff to get his gun out – he killed both Tom and Ace.'

'What about you?' asked Jane in a whisper.

'I was on top of him before he could shoot

again,' replied Vance, 'and this enabled me to get away. It was some days later before I was caught.'

'If you hadn't knocked Tom's arm...' began Jane.

'We'd hev all been wanted as murderers,' put in Vance quickly, 'an' I believe death the way it came was better than at the end of a rope. Believe me,' he went on, a pleading look in his eyes, 'I didn't want it to happen that way, but once you start killing lawmen there's no goin' back, thet's why Ace an' I were always careful about this.'

Vance waited for Jane's reaction. He could almost sense the turmoil in her mind.

'Why did he do it? It wouldn't have mattered coming back with nothing,' Jane whispered half to herself.

'He did it because he loved you,' said Vance quietly. 'I'm to blame. I shouldn't hev expected a young drover to be an experienced bank robber but...'

'You did it to help him, Vance,' cut in Jane sympathetically.

'But I was also the cause of his death,' replied Vance.

'That was a risk he took,' said Jane. 'I have no doubt you briefed him carefully on what to do.'

'I don't know what to say,' said Vance. He was surprised at her calmness.

'There is no need to tell you that this has been a great shock to me,' said Jane softly, 'but somehow I didn't feel anything. I have been expecting to hear that Tom was dead and, you see, I know he really wasn't a bank robber – he never could be and the fact that my feelings for you have grown as they have over the past few weeks all seem to ease the pain that I suppose should be there.'

'Don't, Jane,' pleaded Vance. 'You can't feel anythin' towards me now, knowin' this.'

'I do,' replied Jane. 'Since you came to Plainview I seem to have been building up another life; I love you, Vance, and even this news is not going to break that love. As a matter of fact somehow I feel glad that you and Tom knew each other.'

'But you can't want me now,' said Vance. 'Every time you looked at me you would see the man who had caused your husband's death.'

'No, Vance, I wouldn't,' cried Jane.

'I have everything planned,' put in Vance before Jane could say any more. 'I thought a lot about it when I was in jail. I was determined to find a new life and help the dependants of Ace and Tom. When I came out of prison I learned that Ace had got married a few days before he met me near Cheyenne Wells. I found his widow in New Mexico. Now I have found you I can get everything settled. I will split the money between both of you, that will mean you will have about thirty thousand dollars coming to you.'

Jane gasped. 'Thirty thousand!'

'Yes,' went on Vance. 'I will sell the Running J and leave, it would not be fair to you if I stayed around here.'

Jane looked hard at Vance for a few moments before she spoke. 'And don't I have a say in the matter?' she asked haughtily. 'First of all,' she went on without waiting for Vance to answer the question, 'there is no reason whatsoever for you to leave; this is the place you chose to settle, to go straight, so here you should stay, besides I want you to. Secondly, I don't want the money. I'm comfortably off with the café and wouldn't know what to do with that amount.'

'But don't you see...' began Vance.

'I want no part of it,' broke in Jane firmly. 'I won't touch a dollar of that money. If you did the right thing, Vance, you would give it back.'

'I can't do that when there are two people

179

whom I could help,' replied Vance. 'Please take it, Jane.'

Jane shook her head. 'No! I don't want it.' From the tone of her voice Vance knew it was useless to pursue the matter.

'But I must see that Ace's widow gets her share,' he said. 'Besides, I'll have to leave here; these men who are after the money will follow and then there will be no more danger to anyone around here.'

'Don't you see that the best thing is to give it all back,' pleaded Jane. 'You'll have to take lawmen with you then, these three men won't dare act and once it is back in safe hands they won't bother you again.'

Vance smiled wryly. 'I think you under-estimate the lengths to which men will go to get that amount of money,' he said. 'Besides, there is Della Jenkins, I owe it to her.' Vance went on to tell Jane, Della's story, and when he had finished she saw it was useless to try to persuade him otherwise, but already she was formulating a plan to help Vance.

'Very well,' she said, 'I see your mind is made up, but please, Vance, don't sell the Running J. I would like to share my life with you.'

Vance smiled. 'All right,' he agreed. 'I won't think about selling until I have settled this other matter. You have been so under-standing, Jane, and I am grateful to you, but we'll see if you still feel the same way when I return.'

'When will you go?' she asked.

'I'll go back to the ranch tonight, then I will be ready to leave first thing in the morn-ing.'

When Brady left her house Jane waited five minutes before throwing a shawl around her shoulders and hurrying to the sheriff's house intending to tell him of Vance's inten-tions but, much to her consternation, she learned that the sheriff had left town and was not likely to be back until the following morning.

Mel Walker, Wes Carter and Butch Nolan sought safety in the darkness as they galloped away from the Running J leaving Vance Brady to be discovered by the unknown arrivals. After they had travelled about a mile Mel Walker called a halt. They listened for sounds of pursuit and, when he was satisfied that they had not been followed, Mel reassessed the position.

'I reckon Brady wouldn't have talked,' he said, 'but it may well cause him to move from here and dispose of the Cheyenne

Wells money quickly. I think we must keep an even closer watch on him from now on. We'll head back for the Running J and keep an eye on developments.'

Neither of the other men questioned Mel's decision and before long they were approaching the ranch-house cautiously. A short while later they saw three figures emerge from the house and head in the direction of Plainview.

'Looks as if they are taking Brady into town,' whispered Wes.

'Right,' said Mel, 'I think you had better stay here, Wes, keep an eye on the ranch. I figure if Brady decides to go after that cash he'll probably come back here first. Butch and I will keep an eye on things in town.'

Wes nodded and settled down for the night whilst Walker and Nolan followed the three riders into town. When they entered Plainview Mel and his sidekick proceeded with the utmost caution and once they saw that Brady appeared to be staying at the sheriff's house they made their way to the saloon where they informed Mavis Cameron of the developments.

Throughout the following day she kept as close a check on Brady's movements as she could and when she reported that he was visiting Jane Elliot in the evening Mel sent

Butch to keep a watch on the house. When Vance left Jane's Butch followed him until he was satisfied that Brady was heading for the Running J and then returned to the saloon to report to Walker.

'Good work,' congratulated Mel. 'Now it's up to Carter. He's had a long wait but it may pay off.'

Wes Carter spent an uneasy day when Vance Brady did not return to the Running J and he began to think that maybe Mel Walker had double-crossed him. He realised his position was a bit precarious and finally decided he would stay another night. As darkness fell across the Texas countryside Wes moved closer to the house and was thankful he had done so when he heard the clop of a horse's hoofs approaching. He was relieved when he recognised Vance Brady and when Vance took his horse to the stable Wes knew he would be spending the night at the Running J.

The following morning Wes was awake early and excitement seized him when, about mid-morning, he saw Vance, carrying two packs, come out of the house and go to the stable. Ten minutes later Brady re-appeared with his horse and Wes watched him carefully as he rode away heading in a northerly direction. Wes followed him until he felt satisfied that Vance was settled on a definite trail northwards. Mel had been right; Brady was on the move. Carter pulled his horse round and put it into a fast gallop towards Plainview.

Sheriff Jed Owen was heading across country towards the trail for Plainview when, on topping a small rise, he suddenly pulled his horse to a halt. A cloud of dust billowed behind a rider in the distance and the sheriff read it as a sign of a man on an urgent mission. Jed pulled out his spyglass and drew the rider into focus.

'Wes Carter!' Jed gasped to himself. He frowned. Vance had said that he was certain one of his attackers had been Carter and now here he was alone on a trail which he could easily have reached from the Running J. Could he have come from there? Was he going to contact his accomplices?

Jed pushed his horse forward determined at all costs to follow Carter to his destination. Wes was so intent on his ride that he did not notice the lawman slip on to the trail and follow at a safe distance. Jed was surprised when Carter showed no sign of deviating from the trail to Plainview and, when the meaning of this struck him he cursed himself for not thinking that the three men might be hiding out under his very nose in Plainview. So this was why they had been able to keep a close check on Brady's activities, but even so he knew they must have an accomplice in town. Determined not to lose sight of Carter he closed the gap as they neared the town where he trailed him carefully through the streets to the back of the Golden Cage. When he saw the bounty hunter enter the building he moved forward quickly and was just in time to hear a door shut on the upper floor as he stepped inside the back door. Jed moved up the stairs quickly and crept quietly along the corridor listening carefully. He paused against a door where he heard voices and, although he recognised Carter's voice, the conversation was in low tones so that he could not catch the words. Suddenly he realised what the set-up must have been and had to admire the coolness of the scheme. Mavis Cameron, whom he knew had been sweet on Carter, had kept track of Brady possibly through his men when they visited the saloon.

He was tempted to burst into the room but he realised he had nothing on these men and that he would have to play a waiting game. He started to move along the corridor to the stairs but his decision had come too late. The door of the room opened and Wes Carter stepped out. Although he was surprised at seeing someone in the corridor Wes drew his Colt in a flash, and by the time Jed had spun round he found himself staring into a cold muzzle.

'Hold it!' rapped Wes. His eyes widened when he saw the sheriff then, knowing he had the upper hand, he relaxed. 'Wal, if it isn't the sheriff,' he called, loud enough so that Mel and Butch would hear and stay out of sight. 'Doin' a bit of snoopin'?' he asked as he stepped forward and pulled the sheriff's Colt from its holster. Suddenly he jerked his gun upwards and brought it crashing down on Jed's temple. The lawman staggered backwards against the wall and slid to the floor in a heap. 'Butch,' called Wes, and when Nolan appeared he told him to drag the sheriff into the room.

'Wonder how much he heard?' said Mel, then shrugged his shoulder. 'Wal, it doesn't matter; we never mentioned where we were going so when he comes round he won't know whether we've ridden north, south, east or west.'

'He must hev followed me into town,'

mused Wes, 'but he still hasn't seen you two. Mavis, this hombre's a smart sheriff; I guess he might put two and two together; I reckon you'd better leave on the next stage. I'll meet you in Abilene.'

Butch found some rope and quickly bound and gagged the sheriff. When he had finished Mel turned to Mavis.

'If he comes round he won't bother you. Lock him in when you leave.'

'I'll be out of this town in half an hour,' replied Mavis with a smile.

The three men left the saloon and were soon heading away from Plainview along the north trail.

Twenty minutes later Mavis, after gathering her few belongings together, locked the door of her room, hurried from the saloon by the back entrance and made her way quickly to the stage office. She paid her fare and boarded the coach a few minutes before it pulled out of Plainview.

Jed Owen stirred. His head throbbed from the hard blow and consciousness returned only slowly. As his brain cleared he was staggered to find himself securely bound and gagged. He struggled with his bonds but only succeeded in making his head pound all the more. Jed struggled across the floor inch by inch until he reached the door. He managed to push himself upwards until, with his back to the door, he was able to grip the knob. He turned it with great difficulty but found the door unyielding. Suddenly his grip slipped and he fell forward with a crash, banging his head on the floor. His brain spun as he lay in a half-daze. Gradually his senses returned and he looked round desperately for some means of trying to cut through his ropes. Seeing nothing, he shuffled forward, feet first, to the door. Jed kicked hard at the door and, in spite of the hardness of the effort from such an awkward position, kept kicking at it, hoping to attract someone's attention. Minutes passed and the sheriff was almost giving up when he heard feet hurrying along the corridor.

'What's goin' on in there,' yelled a gruff voice.

Jed replied by kicking the door again. He saw the knob turn and someone try the door. Suddenly there was a crash, the door flew open, and the barman staggered into the room, almost falling over the sheriff. He gasped with surprise when he saw Jed and quickly untied him.

'What's happened?' he gasped.

'It's a long story,' replied Jed rubbing his

wrists and ankles vigorously. 'I'll tell you all about it later. Hev you seen Mavis?'

The barman shook his head. 'I heven't but someone came in the saloon and said they'd seen her get on the stage which left a quarter of an hour ago.'

Jed cursed and pushed himself to his feet. He staggered and supported himself against the wall. There was concern on the barman's face as he suggested he should get the doctor.

Jed shook his head. 'No time,' he said. 'A whisky will help when we get down stairs.'

The two men left the room and once they reached the bar the bartender quickly poured a whisky which Jed drained in one gulp. It seemed to drive some life into the lawman and, after reassuring the barman that he would be all right, he left the Golden Cage.

He crossed the dusty street to his office and when he reached the door he heard someone running along the sidewalk. He stopped, glanced round and was surprised to see Jane Elliot, a worried look on her face, running towards him.

'I'm glad you're back,' she panted as she reached him. Her eyes widened; a look of concern crossed her face when she saw the ugly gash across Jed's temple. 'What happened? Are you all right?'

Jed nodded. 'I'll be all right,' he said. 'I think the hombres who hev been worryin' Vance hev gone, but you look troubled, what's the matter?'

'Vance has left,' answered Jane. 'He figured if he rode out of here the trouble would follow him.'

Jed gasped. 'Then thet's why those hombres hev pulled out, thet's why Carter was in such a hurry to git to town, he must hev been keepin' an eye on Vance.'

He opened the office door. 'Come inside, Jane,' he said, 'and tell me what happened.'

Jane told her story quickly and they fitted Jed's experiences into it.

'Vance is in great danger,' said Jane. 'We've got to do something to help him.'

'I'll go after him,' replied Jed.

'But you aren't fit,' said Jane. 'And you don't know where he's going.'

'I hev a good idea he'll head for Wagon Mound,' said Jed with a smile. 'Don't worry, I'll be all right when I git patched up.'

'When you catch up with Vance try and persuade him to return that money,' pleaded Jane. 'I don't want any of it.'

The sheriff smiled as he walked to the

door. 'I'll do my best,' he promised.

An hour later Jed Owen had been attended to by the doctor and was taking the north road out of Plainview.

Chapter Twelve

When Vance Brady left the Running J his thoughts were in a turmoil. He had thought he could find happiness in Plainview and would be able to forget his old life once he disposed of the Cheyenne Wells money, but his past had come sharply before him in Jane Elliot, the girl with whom he had fallen in love. Vance cursed his luck. If only Jane had not been Corby's widow, and yet she had said she loved him. Vance did not know what to do about the future; that would have to take care of itself; at the moment he was doing the only thing he figured he could do – leave Plainview and hope his troubles would follow him.

He made no attempt to disguise his leaving; he reckoned that these men were so desperate to get the money they would be keeping a close watch on every move. However, it was not until the following afternoon that he knew with any certainty that he was being followed. His hand strayed to his saddle-bag and felt his gunbelt. There was some reassurance in its feel and Vance was tempted to strap it on, but he knew that there was time enough before he need do that.

It was during the same afternoon that Jed Owen, who had kept a steady pace after leaving Plainview, sighted three riders some distance ahead. He studied them intently through his spy-glass as they rode up a long rise. Seeing Wes Carter he knew these were the men he wanted, but the other two he had not seen before. As he watched them he realised that he would have to play this thing carefully. He guessed that Vance would not be very far ahead and he was tempted to ride ahead and join Brady but recognised that this might have the wrong effect; Jed wanted to make sure that Vance was not harmed and at the same time be reassured that he was wanted back in Plainview, and Jed was prepared to play a waiting game to achieve this.

Three days later, as they were heading through the mountains of New Mexico, Jed was surprised to see one of the three riders suddenly leave the other two and head to the right. Jed realised he had only a split second to make up his mind what to do. If he followed the lone rider it might take him away from Vance; on the other hand the man might be wanting to get ahead of Brady for some reason and Jed felt sure that he would not be leaving everything to his two companions. His decision made Jed pull his horse round and, using every means of cover, headed on a trail parallel to that of the lone rider.

As Mel Walker guessed, Vance Brady was heading for Wagon Mound, and now that he was certain of this Mel decided it would be better if he saw Della Jenkins before Vance Brady.

Once Walker crossed over a ridge into a valley he put his horse into a fast gallop and Jed, realising that Walker was out-riding Brady, matched his pace to the man ahead determined to keep him in sight at all costs. Mile after mile Walker kept to this pace and Jed was somewhat relieved when he topped a rise and saw Wagon Mound nestling in a valley below. Walker was already pounding along the trail to town and Jed realised he must keep close if he wanted to find out who the man was and why he was in such a hurry to get to Wagon Mound.

When they reached the main street Walker slowed to a trot and Jed knew he would have to be careful for it was more than likely that the man ahead would recognise him as the sheriff from Plainview. When he saw Walker pull his horse to the rails outside the saloon Jed halted, swung from the saddle, hitched his horse to the rail and sauntered along the sidewalk. When Walker entered the saloon Jed quickened his pace and reached a window in time to see a young woman hurry across the saloon to meet Walker. She seemed pleased to see him and after a brief exchange of words Jed saw them leave the main room by a door which he guessed led to rooms at the back.

Jed's thoughts raced. Had Walker merely hurried ahead to see this woman? If so, then when would...? Suddenly Jed started. This must be the widow of Ace Jenkins. Vance had said she worked in a saloon in Wagon Mound. She was associating with a man whom he knew was after the Cheyenne Wells money, then she must be in this with him! Jed realised he must get nearer to the truth for Vance's sake. He hurried round the building where he estimated the first two windows let into the bar. He crept stealthily to the third and peered cautiously inside, but the room was empty. Moving on to the next window he heard voices and seeing the bottom of the window was slightly open he crouched below it. Removing his sombrero, he raised his head slowly, and excitement seized him when he saw the man he had been trailing sitting behind a large desk and smiling at the girl who looked somewhat worried.

'Don't look so troubled,' Jed heard him say. 'Everything will turn out all right. We forced Brady to move. Butch and another hombre name of Wes Carter are on his tail but I just had to ride ahead to see you, honey.' He smiled.

'Mel, I've been frightened, you've been away so long,' said the girl.

Walker pushed himself to his feet and walked to the girl. He held her firmly by the shoulders.

'Has Brady got the money?' asked the girl.

Walker shook his head. 'No, but I'm certain he's on his way to get it,' he replied. 'I reckon he's coming through here to reassure you he's not forgotten you.'

'Then let's settle for my share,' said Della urgently.

Walker's face darkened. 'Not now,' he said

sharply. 'We've gone this far, we'll go the whole way and get the lot. Don't forget you don't owe Brady any sympathy; Ace would be alive today if it wasn't for him, you would still be Mrs Jenkins and would never have had to seek a living the way you did. Don't miss this opportunity to take Brady for the lot and you'll have everything you want.'

'I guess you're right,' replied Della. 'I'm sorry, but I suppose it was with you being away so long. I had visions of you being dead and I having to go back to that way of living ... well, you know what I mean, Mel.'

Walker kissed her. 'No more worrying,' he said. 'Play this right and we'll soon be rich. Get any information you can out of Brady. I'll keep out of sight again, it will make it easier to take him.' He went on to explain his association with Carter and their plans.

When he was satisfied that he had heard all that would be of use to him Jed Owen slipped away from the window and, after taking the horse to the livery stable, he went to the hotel, booked a room which gave him a view of the main street, and enquired about the owner of the saloon.

He felt inclined to contact Vance when he arrived in Wagon Mound and to tell him how Ace Jenkins' widow was teamed with the owner of the saloon to get their hands on all of the Cheyenne Wells money, but he realised Vance would probably not believe him. Somehow he had to show the Jenkins woman in her true light. That, coupled with the fact that Jane Elliot wanted none of the money might persuade Vance to return it to the proper authorities.

The light was fading when Vance Brady rode slowly into Wagon Mound. There were lights in several windows, a piano strummed tunelessly from the saloon, shrieks of laughter came from an open window, and several miners, who had obviously been in town most of the day, staggered along the sidewalk bent on returning to the saloon. Vance pulled his horse to a halt outside the livery stable unaware that two men had just ridden into Main Street and a third watched him intently from a darkened window in the hotel. Brady led his horse into the stable and a few moments later reappeared to walk towards the hotel. Jed Owen stiffened when he saw Wes Carter and Butch Nolan ride slowly past to pull up outside the saloon and disappear inside.

Nolan led Carter straight to Walker's room.

'He's jest gone into the hotel,' said Nolan,

'looks as if he's goin' to stay the night.'

'Good,' said Mel. 'You can both get some sleep tonight, a room down the corridor you can use but whatever you do keep out of sight, I'll send in anything you want.'

'Aren't we goin' to keep an eye on Brady?' protested Carter.

Walker smiled. 'Somebody will watch him, I want you two refreshed and ready to ride as soon as Brady pulls out.'

The door opened and Della hurried in. 'What's happening?' she asked anxiously. 'I only just got away from the cards.'

'Brady's booked in at the hotel,' explained Mel. 'No doubt you'll see him before long, you know what to do.'

Della nodded and a few moments later returned to the saloon. Her mind was hardly on the game as she played cards and she kept watching the door anxiously. An hour passed before the batwings were pushed open and Vance Brady strolled in. Della concentrated on the game appearing as though she had not noticed him. She was aware that he was walking towards her table.

'Evenin', Laura, or should I say Della?' Vance's voice was quiet.

Della looked up. Surprise crossed her face. 'Vance Brady!' she gasped. 'I'd given you up for lost.'

'I said I'd be back,' replied Vance as he sat down at the table. 'Sorry,' he added turning to the miner who was playing the cards, 'I'll wait.' He watched Della closely as she continued the game. He realised how much she must have changed since those days in Greely. In fact he reckoned people there would not recognise her now. Vance detected a hardness about her, detected a ruthlessness in her game which he figured she would certainly turn to her advantage if the cards started going the wrong way. He knew the money which was coming from him would never change her way of life. In fact he thought it would, in all probability, put her in deeper. He began to wonder if he was right in what he proposed to do, but he had made a promise. Vance wished the miner would pull out of the game for he found himself comparing Jane and Della and it disturbed him.

Eventually the miner had lost enough and stopped playing. Before someone else could take his place Della called one of the other girls over to play for her. Della led Vance to a table in a corner and when the barman had brought some drinks she looked at Vance.

'Have you come to settle your agreement?'

she asked.

'Not yet,' replied Vance quietly.

Della looked surprised. 'What!' she gasped. 'What are you doing here?'

'I came to reassure you that I had not forgotten you,' said Vance. 'I'm on my way to collect the money now. It took some time to find the widow of the cowboy I told you about.'

'You found her?' asked Della.

'Yes,' answered Vance. 'I figure on splitting the money between you.'

'What about you?' queried Della.

'I'm not bothered for myself,' replied Vance. He hesitated a moment then looked searchingly at Della. 'Do you think this is right?' he asked. 'Do you think I should give the money back to the authorities?'

'What!' Della was taken aback. Her eyes flashed. 'What's got into you, Brady, going soft? Don't let me down now, I want that money, want it bad, so don't get stupid ideas. Don't forget you were responsible for what happened to me,' she cried angrily. 'If you hadn't saved that lawman Ace would probably be alive.'

'All right, all right,' said Vance urgently. 'You'll get your money; I'll keep my bargain; I just wondered.'

'Well don't,' snapped Della. 'Just get it here, the sooner the better.'

'It won't be long now,' replied Vance. 'I'll pull out early in the morning an' be back in about three days.' He pulled himself from the table and bade her goodnight.

As soon as Vance was through the bat-wings Della hurried to one of Walker's side-kicks who was leaning on the bar.

'Follow that man,' she instructed, 'he's likely to be staying the night at the hotel. Let Mel know the moment he looks like leaving town.'

The man nodded, drained his glass and hurried from the saloon. He saw Vance Brady some distance along the sidewalk and he sauntered along in the same direction. When Brady crossed the street towards the hotel the man stopped and leaned on the rail until he saw him enter the building. He then stepped from the sidewalk, crossed the dusty road and peered through the window of the hotel. He saw Brady going up the stairs so he flopped into a chair beside the door, rolled himself a cigarette and settled down to await Brady's reappearance.

Jed Owen was relieved when he saw Vance Brady come out of the saloon, but a moment later the tension returned when he saw a man push through the batwings and follow Brady. Jed's thoughts raced. Was this man merely keeping an eye on Brady or was there something more sinister in his movements? He watched the man until he passed from view below him. Jed moved swiftly to the door of his room. He heard footsteps up the stairs and when they passed his door he opened it slightly and saw that the person was Brady. Once Vance had entered his room Jed slipped quickly down the stairs. The man who had followed Brady was not in the lobby so Jed crossed to the outside door and stepped out on to the sidewalk. Relief swept him when he saw a man sitting in a chair beside the door. Jed strolled along the street and when he returned a short while later the man was still there.

Before going upstairs Jed asked the clerk to arrange for breakfast things to be brought to his room early the following morning. Although this was an unusual request the clerk did not protest when Jed slipped him a tip and even went so far as to say that he would bring the meal over from the café personally.

Daylight had just flooded into Wagon Mound when Jed Owen dressed quickly and took up his position beside the window. He was still there when the clerk appeared with his breakfast. After the man had gone Jed took the tray to a table in front of the window so that he was able to watch the street and have his meal at the same time. Five minutes later he heard footsteps pass along the corridor and go down the stairs. In a few moments Vance Brady crossed the street, entered the café, and half an hour later hurried along the sidewalk to the livery stable. As soon as he had disappeared inside the building the man who had kept the all-night vigil outside the hotel ran across the street to the saloon. Jed now saw events unfold swiftly. Vance came out of the livery stable leading his horse and crossed the street to the hotel. Jed heard him come up to his room and a few moments later he saw three men whom he recognised as Mel Walker, Butch Nolan and Wes Carter appear with their horses in a side street next to the saloon. The man who had kept watch on Brady strolled from the saloon and lounged at the corner of the building. Jed heard Vance leave his room and hurry down the stairs and a few moments later when he saw the man on the corner signal to the three men along the side street he knew

Vance had left the building. A few moments later Vance moved into view as he rode slowly along Main Street.

Suddenly Jed stiffened. Vance Brady was wearing a gun!

Chapter Thirteen

Jed was shaken out of his surprise when Vance put his horse into a trot. He glanced across the street and saw the man on the corner give another signal. Mel Walker and his two companions rode slowly on to the main street and turned in the direction taken by Vance Brady. As soon as they were out of sight the Sheriff of Plainview moved swiftly into action. He grabbed his belongings, hurried downstairs, paid the clerk and quickly crossed the street to the livery stable. A few minutes later he too took the north road out of Wagon Mound and once he sighted the three men matched his pace to theirs.

Vance Brady rode steadily throughout the day along the main trail through the mountainous country towards Raton Pass. He knew that before long there would have to be a showdown with the three men whom he knew were following him and with this in mind he realised it would be to his advantage to get a closer look at them. He chose his camp for the night carefully. He did not bother with a fire and laid his blankets out between two huge boulders a short distance from the trail. Knowing he would be watched he made a pretence of bedding down as the light was fading. As soon as it was dark he slipped out of his blankets and using boulders as cover he gradually worked his way up the hillside to his right until he had a commanding view of the direction from which he had come that day. He smiled to himself when he saw the gleam of a fire. This was just what he had hoped for. He worked his way slowly and carefully towards the glow and as he neared it he realised it was in a slight hollow, and had he not climbed the hillside he would never have seen it. He crept to the edge of the incline, keeping himself as flat as possible. He found himself looking down on the camp where the three men were seated round the fire having a meal. Vance recognised Wes Carter but the other two he had not seen before. As he studied them carefully their voices drifted to him on the still night air.

'We've got to keep our eye on him through-out the night,' instructed one of the men.

'There's no need,' replied Carter irritably, 'I've seen him bed down, he's obviously settled for the night.'

'We must be getting near the place where he hid that money,' came the reply. 'We are not going to miss out on it now, just for the sake of keeping an extra watch on Brady. I'm in charge of this, so we'll do it my way; what you do after you take Brady is your business.'

Vance smiled to himself and slid silently away from the hollow back to his bed roll where he settled down for the night.

The following morning he was up early and, after a quick breakfast, was in the saddle climbing steadily towards Raton Pass. Shortly after noon he crossed the pass and moved westwards off the main trail. The terrain was not so familiar to him but he reckoned that once he crossed the next three ridges he would be in the long depression which he was seeking.

The ground became rougher and the three men had to close the gap to keep Vance in sight. Jed Owen had a feeling that when they swung off the trail they must be nearing the place where Vance had hidden the money.

He decided that he must get closer to Brady so that he could keep both hunter and hunted within his sight. Accordingly he swung in an arc which took him wide of the three men, and, in this rough country, it was an easy matter to keep out of sight. The result was that when Jed saw Vance ride down into the depression he found himself still with plenty of cover on the west side of the hollow. He moved steadily forward, keeping pace with Vance as he rode on. Glancing back Jed saw the three men had pulled to a halt behind some boulders on the edge of the flatness. He realised they had been caught without cover to use and if they moved forward Brady would see them.

Mel Walker cursed when he realised that they would have to wait until Brady left the hollow. The gap would be widened and Brady might give them the slip, but there was nothing they could do but wait. Anger darkened Carter's face; he could see Brady escaping and it took a lot of persuasion by Mel Walker to prevent him from riding after Brady.

Vance started to climb the slope at the far end of the hollow when suddenly he swung to the left along the hillside towards the cave he had last visited nearly five years ago. He knew that his objective was probably clear to the men who were trailing him but he realised that he would be in a very strong position from which to take on three men.

As soon as Brady altered his track Walker pulled out his spyglass. He drew the rider into focus then slowly moved the glass ahead, studying the ground to try to spot the reason for Brady's move. Suddenly he stopped and a gasp of triumph came from him.

'I've got it!' he cried. 'Brady's making for a cave; the money must be hidden there!'

'Good,' called Wes. 'Let's go.'

'Hold it,' snapped Walker. 'Across that hollow we'd be sitting targets for a man up there. You and I will work our way to the left. Butch, you go to the right and move in on Brady whilst we keep him pinned down; you'll have to move fast, you've more ground to cover.'

Nolan nodded, pulled his horse round and rode to the right using as much cover as possible as he swung under the hillside to work round to the cave. Walker and Carter started to the left, keeping a careful watch on Brady all the time.

Jed Owen had also spotted the cave and when he saw the three men make a move he slipped from the saddle and led his horse up the slope where he secured it out of sight behind a group of huge rocks. Pulling his Colt from its holster he moved a short distance down the hillside and awaited developments.

Vance was almost at the cave and, whilst Nolan had made good progress on the far side of the hollow, Walker and Carter were moving quickly along the hillside a little below Jed. They passed below the sheriff and halted a little further along the hillside. Slipping from their saddles they waited until they saw Nolan turn towards the cave. When they started to creep forward Jed moved after them. Vance had entered the cave but so far had not reappeared, and when they had reached a position close to the entrance to the cave, Walker was puzzled by this fact.

He waited a few minutes and when he saw Nolan climb from his horse and start to work his way along the hillside he was prepared to make the first move, but the decision was taken from his hands. Vance had found the money quickly and settled down to wait for his pursuers to make the play, but as the minutes passed he began to wonder if he had been wrong. Maybe he had lost them in the rough country since crossing Raton

Pass. Certainly he had not been aware of them for some time; maybe they had not been as smart as he had expected. He grew impatient and realised there was only one way to find out. Picking up the bag he moved cautiously to the entrance to the cave. As soon as he appeared Carter raised his gun but Walker stopped him.

'Let him come out,' he whispered, 'then Butch will be able to get the drop on him from behind.'

Both men watched intently as Vance moved slowly into the open. When he was half-way between the cave and a small group of rocks Walker called out.

'Hold it, Brady!' he shouted. 'You're covered. Just throw that bag over and you'll be free to go.'

For a moment Vance froze. They had tested his patience and he had fallen for it. He must be slipping, but then he knew it was a desire to get this thing over, to get the money to Della Jenkins and a chance of seeing Jane Elliot again that had really tried his patience. Suddenly Vance moved into action, flinging himself forward towards the group of rocks. A bullet rang close to his head as he did so and another whined off the rock in front of him as he hit the ground and rolled over. The force of the impact broke his grip on the bag which spun out of his hand and rolled a few yards down the hillside. Once behind the rocks his Colt leaped to his hand and, easing it round the edge of a boulder, he fired twice in the direction from which the bullets had come at him. He ducked behind the rocks as two more bullets cracked unpleasantly close to his head. He saw the position was not very advantageous, somehow he had to draw these men into the open. His thoughts raced and suddenly hit on a plan which he knew was desperate and which would test whether or not he had lost any of his speed of draw over the years. He pushed his gun back into its holster.

'All right,' he shouted. 'You've got the drop on me. I'm coming out.'

Walker grinned at Carter. 'We've done it,' he said. Excitement had seized him, a fortune could be in his hands in a few moments. His cool reasoning had suddenly vanished and as Brady stepped into the open Walker broke cover to meet him. Carter, suspicious of Brady's move, waited a moment and when Brady appeared his Colt covered him. When Vance saw only Walker appear he knew that his supposition that all three men, their judgment lost in the excitement of triumph, would automatically appear had been wrong. His position was desperate and Brady took desperate measures.

He dived forward, jerking at his Colt as he did so. Before he hit the ground his finger had squeezed the trigger and the bullet hit Walker high on the chest sending him crashing backwards. As soon as Carter saw Brady move he fired but his bullet only sent Brady's sombrero flying from his head. His finger was already squeezing the trigger again when there was a roar behind him. Carter never knew who fired the bullet which ploughed into his back, and as he pitched forward his own Colt roared harmlessly into the ground.

The whole action had been so swift that it had taken Nolan by surprise, but there was Brady laid on the ground, a target which he couldn't miss. He leaped upright from his cover, his Colt coming down towards Vance.

'Behind you, Vance!' yelled Jed, almost as soon as he had killed Carter.

Automatically Vance rolled over and Nolan's bullet took him in the left arm. Before Butch could fire again Vance's Colt roared, catching Nolan high on the right

212

shoulder. Nolan staggered, his Colt roared again but his aim had been spoilt and before he could take another shot Vance's bullet hit him in the heart. He pitched to the ground and lay still. The silence which suddenly followed the crescendo was almost frightening. Vance half expected Colts to start roaring again, then he realised someone had shouted. His arm hurt but he pushed himself to his feet. He gasped with surprise when he saw the Sheriff of Plainview, gun in hand, running towards him.

'Jed!' he said incredulously. 'What are you doing here? How did…?'

'I've been followin' ever since these hombres left Plainview. Tell you all about it shortly.'

'Then it was you who fired that shot from over there,' said Vance.

'Sure,' replied Jed. 'Carter fired when you came to meet Walker but you had dived forward. He had you lined up for the kill with his next shot but he was never able to fire it.'

'Thanks,' said Vance gratefully, 'an' thanks for the warning about thet other hombre, you hed them all taped. You said one of them was called Walker. Know anythin' about them?'

'Walker an' his sidekick Nolan are from Wagon Mound,' said Jed.

'Wagon Mound!' gasped Vance. 'But they've been followin' me since I left Plainview.'

'Thet's right,' said Jed. 'They teamed up with Wes Carter. I reckon they trailed you when you came south and met up with Carter somewhere along the line. You'll probably git all the answers in Cheyenne Wells.'

'Cheyenne Wells?' Vance was both surprised and curious. Suspicion crossed his mind. He looked at Jed wryly. 'You said if ever you got your hands on the money you'd turn it over to the authorities,' he went on quietly. 'You've followed me for that purpose. But I mean to take thet cash to Wagon Mound.'

Jed, realising the thoughts which must be racing through Brady's mind, raised his Colt to cover his friend. 'I'm sorry, Vance,' he said. 'I know what you must be thinkin', believe me that was not the purpose of my trip. I knew you were in danger and Jane was concerned about you; we both want you back in Plainview.'

There was doubt in Vance's mind. 'I can't go back to Plainview,' he said. 'It couldn't work out for Jane and I knowin' about Tom

Corby. I'm goin' to split the Cheyenne Wells money between Jane and Ace Jenkins' widow; you're a lawman, Jed, it's only natural you should want to recover the money, but don't try to stop me.'

Vance took a step forward, but Jed's gun menaced him.

'Don't try it, Vance!' rapped the lawman. 'You've got to come to Cheyenne Wells fer your own good. Trust me,' he pleaded. 'We've been good friends since you came to Plainview. You've a chance to settle down there and Jane's more interested in you than the money. Believe me you've got to come to Cheyenne Wells, your future depends on it.'

Vance looked at Jed curiously. There was a sincerity about this man which he liked, which made him feel he had to play along with him, and yet he was first and foremost a lawman. Jed could sense the doubt in Vance's mind.

'Look here, Vance,' he went on. 'To show my trust in you I'll holster my gun an' you'd be able to take me any time you wanted – you're faster on the draw than I am, but I don't think you'll do it because I believe that you've the good sense to know that I wouldn't get you to Cheyenne Wells under false pretences.' The sheriff holstered his gun and the two men faced each other without speaking.

Vance stared at Jed. His thoughts tumbled. He was attracted by Plainview; Jane had said she loved him and wanted no money, but he had Della Jenkins to think about. He could outdraw Jed Owen and get clean away and yet he felt there was something deeper in Jed's request to go to Cheyenne Wells. He looked at the sheriff shrewdly.

'Why do you want me to go to Cheyenne Wells?' he asked.

Jed smiled. 'If I told you, you wouldn't believe me; it's something you must find out for yourself.'

'Very well,' said Vance. 'Let's go.'

Jed picked up the bag and the two men collected their horses and were soon heading in the direction of the Arkansas River. They crossed this close to Rocky Ford and the following afternoon were riding into Cheyenne Wells.

'I guess it will be straight to your brother,' said Vance as they rode up the dusty main street.

'The hotel first,' replied Jed.

Thinking they were going to book rooms for the night Vance said nothing and followed Jed into the hotel. The clerk looked up as the two men approached the desk.

'Good day, gentlemen,' he greeted with a smile.

'Hev you a lady staying here by the name of Laura or maybe Della Jenkins?' asked Jed.

Vance gasped with surprise. He looked at Jed incredulously. 'What the…?'

'Yes,' answered the clerk. 'Room twelve, she's been expecting visitors.'

'Thank you,' said Jed and hurried to the stairs before Vance could say any more.

Vance stared after him for a moment and then followed. His thoughts raced without finding any answer to his questions. When they reached room twelve Jed tapped sharply on the door. They heard someone hurry across the room and the door was flung open to reveal a smiling Della Jenkins.

'Mel, at las…' Her voice trailed away. The smile vanished from her face and she stared unbelievingly at the two men.

Jed stepped past her into the room and Vance followed. Della swung round on the two men. Her eyes were blazing with anger and fury as she stared wildly at Vance.

'You've killed him,' she screamed hatefully. 'My second chance of happiness that you've taken away from me.' She flung herself at Vance, beating him with her fists. Jed grabbed her and pulled her off flinging her on to the bed where she collapsed, sobbing hysterically into the pillow.

Vance stared at Jed. 'She expected Mel Walker,' he whispered.

Jed nodded. 'Mel owned the saloon in Wagon Mound. I learned this when I followed him from Plainview.'

'Then she must hev put him on to me when I was riding south,' said Brady.

'I guess so,' said Jed. 'I overheard them talking and they were not content with what you were goin' to give Della; they were playing for the lot.'

'What about Carter?' asked Vance.

'I don't really know, but I figure they lost your trail and happened to come across Carter who knew where you were,' said Jed.

Vance looked at Della. He stepped towards the bed. 'I'm sorry it turned out this way,' he said. 'If only you...'

Della looked up, hate in her eyes. 'I don't want your pity,' she snapped. 'I wished I'd never heard of you. I wish you'd leave me alone, I don't want your money.'

'You did,' answered Vance, 'but I see it would hev done you no good. I can see now that I was wrong to think I could help two people by just giving them money, they needed more than that and I'm afraid you are beyond help, but I know someone else who isn't. C'm on, Jed, we'll go and see your brother.' Vance hurried from the room and Jed followed.

A few moments later the sheriff of Cheyenne Wells was amazed to see his brother walk into his office with Vance Brady, who handed over some of the money stolen from the bank five years ago. There was bewilderment on his face as he looked at his brother for an explanation.

'It's a long story,' smiled Jed, 'but I guess you'll hev to hear it all.'

'I suppose we'll hev to stay to clear a few things up,' said Vance, 'but I want to be on my way to Plainview and Jane Elliot tomorrow.'

The publishers hope that this book has given you enjoyable reading. Large Print Books are especially designed to be as easy to see and hold as possible. If you wish a complete list of our books please ask at your local library or write directly to:

Dales Large Print Books
Magna House, Long Preston,
Skipton, North Yorkshire.
BD23 4ND

This Large Print Book, for people
who cannot read normal print,
is published under the auspices of

THE ULVERSCROFT FOUNDATION